Accolades for
Remote Control

The Writers Marketing Association's
Indie Excellence Award Winner

"…one part humorous chick lit and one part clever paranormal fantasy, stirred with inspirational wisdom, and served with some startling plot twists. The book you finish is not the same on you started, but you enjoy them both and learn a lot on the journey."

–Tampa Book Buzz

"…an endearing look at the afterlife with wisdom and joy. We come away with the wise admonition to relinquish what we can no longer control…"

–Euro-Reviews

Praise for
Far Above Rubies

"Polansky has written a good and important story here…at times it felt as if Polansky herself was there. The writing is very good…very vivid and well-done…it struck a lot of authentic emotional notes…great job!"

–Writer's Digest

"…Cynthia Polansky skillfully depicts the courage of heart that cannot be broken by man's cruelties…begins with the end, offering a whole picture of life renewed from the ashes of destruction. Polansky tackles this incomprehensible subject with integrity and honesty. Keep a box of Kleenex nearby while reading [it]."

–Women on Writing

REMOTE CONTROL

by

Cynthia Polansky

Echelon Press

Publishing

REMOTE CONTROL

An Echelon Press Book

First Echelon Press paperback printing / November 2007

Front Cover Illustration © Nathalie Moore

www.GraphicsMuse.com

Echelon Press, LLC

9735 Country Meadows Lane 1-D

Laurel, MD 20723

www.echelonpress.com

ISBN 13: 978-1-59080-539-8

ISBN 10: 1-59080-539-9

Library of Congress Control Number: 2007933588

PRINTED IN THE UNITED STATES OF AMERICA

10 9 8 7 6 5 4 3 2 1

For my wonderful husband, Kevin.

Heartfelt thanks go to...

My talented critique group:
Jon Coile, Wendy Sand Eckel, and especially Bridget Bell, without whose help this novel would never have seen daylight.

Karen Syed of Echelon Press,
a publisher every author should be so lucky to snag.

Graphic designer Nathalie Moore
and
editor Kat Thompson,
it really does take a village.

Chick-lit novelist Saralee Rosenberg,
who offered dead-on advice and much-appreciated encouragement.

Mystery/thriller author Austin S. Camacho,
who continues to unselfishly share knowledge that directly contributes to my own success as a writer.

The real Mary Lynn, who inspired this story but isn't evil at all. You just never know what kind of wild ideas will be conceived over dinner at Copeland's...

After all, if the spirit of a loving wife can't nudge her husband in the right direction, who can?

Chapter One

I died on a Tuesday when I was thirty-one years old, in November, my least favorite month in my least favorite season. Bare-naked trees, bleak skies, and twilight falling before the end of *Oprah*. Altogether a depressing time.

Nothing good ever happened to me in autumn. There was the September when I got food poisoning at my aunt's annual Labor Day picnic and spent the remainder of the weekend on my knees before the porcelain god. Or the October I got so frightened by a plastic skeleton dangling over a door at the second-grade's haunted house that I started to cry and all the kids laughed and pointed. And it was November when I chose to shuffle off my mortal coil. *I, Judith Ratner McBride, being of sound mind and body...*make that *being of sound mind...*let's just say I died and leave it at that.

I was nobody extraordinary. Just a nice Jewish physical therapist, happily married to a nice Jewish professional man with an unlikely Irish surname who didn't mind my chunky thighs and frizzy yellow-brown hair. I never won raffles nor was the tenth caller with the correct answer to the radio station's trivia question. So who would have thought my end would come like this?

I know what you must be thinking, but I didn't commit suicide. Yet I did choose to die on that day, in that month, that year, all part of a plan hatched a lifetime ago. But I'll get into all that later.

Somehow I managed to fall into that minuscule percentage of patients who experience one of those possible-but-improbable complications during a routine endoscopy.

Anyone who has ever undergone any kind of invasive medical procedure is familiar with those caveats we tend to gloss over on the required waivers: *This procedure can result in certain complications, including death.* When you really think about it, though, what purpose does the warning serve? If the procedure is necessary, you're going to have it done anyway. And when I died, it's not as though I said to myself, "Well, I can't say they didn't warn me."

In fact, I wasn't even sure what was happening to me, though I did have the proverbial out-of-body experience. I had the sensation of floating out through the top of my head and rising towards the ceiling, watching as the medical team tried to resuscitate me. Staff members began scurrying at once in different directions to their Assigned Responsibilities in the Event of a Life-Threatening Situation.

"I'm not getting a BP, Doctor," reported a nurse.

"One milligram of epinephrine," Dr. Kreske ordered without missing a beat.

The nurse prepared a syringe and plunged it right into

my heart. The team waited and watched as one–forever, it seemed.

"Still no reading, Doctor."

Dr. Kreske's pucker factor must have gone into high gear when epinephrine didn't do the trick. He back-kicked a metal stool out of the way. It rolled into the wall and toppled over with a loud crash, but no one even blinked.

"Begin CPR," Dr. Kreske ordered. A couple of assistants readied the crash cart, while someone else yanked open my hospital gown to lay bare my breast. Once upon a time, I had fantasized about some handsome Jewish doctor doing just that, after which he would sweep me into his strong arms and carry me off to Nordstrom.

Good Dr. Kreske, unmoved by the breasts splayed over the sides of my rib cage, situated the paddles and called out, "Clear!"

I arched an eyebrow at such a dramatic warning. It wasn't as though they stood in front of an airplane propeller.

The electricity made contact, jerking my supine body several inches off the gurney. Five faces looked toward the heart monitor with anticipation that turned to dismay at the persistent flat line. Dr. Kreske once more replaced the paddles and gave his throttle-up warning. My torso arched a little higher, thrusting my bosom upward in a macabre imitation of the seductive pose tempestuous vixens assume while in the throes of ecstasy.

I may have been tempestuous, but I was no vixen and nobody there was ecstatic. About forty minutes later, the team conceded the battle. Time of death was recorded as 1:17 p.m.

The whole situation had been so embarrassing from the start. It wasn't humbling enough in the first place that I had to see a gastroenterologist and describe in great detail my elimination patterns, complete with illustrations. It wasn't sufficient that I, who usually avoided doctors in general, subjected myself to undignified tests while in humiliating, butt-baring positions.

A couple of visits later, I left Dr. Kreske's office with a prescription for a type of laxative new to this child of Generation X-Lax. Oh, I was familiar with over-the-counter pills and the fiber powders stirred into water to concoct a gritty, citrusy beverage, but this stuff resembled something between birdseed and chocolate jimmies. While tempted to feed it to the birds, I was not about to sprinkle it over ice cream. So I did as the label instructed, swallowing a heaping teaspoonful of the dry granules, and chasing it with a full glass of water.

Once in the stomach, the granules were supposed to absorb the water and spur the bowel into action. But the mission was sabotaged by a condition I didn't even know I had. A narrowing of my esophagus caused the granules to bottleneck, unable to proceed to their final destination. Gridlocked at this stricture, they absorbed the water I had drunk until swollen twice their volume, blocking the passage completely. It was like having a matzo ball stuck in your throat that you couldn't get down.

I could still breathe, so I didn't panic. I phoned Dr. Kreske's office, feeling silly and distraught as I explained the problem in between dry heaves. The receptionist told me to have someone bring me to the hospital where Dr. Kreske would 'work me in between procedures.' I knew what *that* meant. He was going to push the offending stuff down with–gulp–an endoscope.

Reluctant to drag my husband Saul away from his office, I knew I could count on my friend Micaela to drive me to the hospital. She had the week off from work, anyway, and said she'd be happy to pinch-hit for Saul.

I worked my way through the hospital's administrative cubicles: one for registration, one for insurance information, one to find out where to go to wait to be told where to go next. At each stop I was obliged to repeat the mortifying explanation of my Ripleyesque problem until at last I was escorted to the procedure room.

They gave me a lovely cocktail of Demerol and Valium which promptly sent me into la-la-land, a desirable place to be when having a large medical implement inserted in your throat. I was grateful for my particular vulnerability to barbiturates (a single antihistamine could knock me out cold), as I didn't want to be the least bit aware of the unwieldy instrument about to send my gag reflexes into overdrive.

When it was all over, the staff tried to rouse me but I didn't respond to repeated attempts. The mood in the room immediately changed from routine to tense. Dr. Kreske maintained an even strain, but I could almost feel the prickle of anxious sweat starting under his arms. Losing me would not be a feather in his surgical cap.

I'm sure no one anticipated such a virulent reaction to the narcotic night-night. Or maybe the barbiturate barkeep poured just wee bit too generously that day. Whatever the reason, the result was the same. But there was a bright side: at least I didn't have to wake up to find a jackhammer down my gullet. As the saying goes, I never knew what hit me.

I had no mystical revelation that I was about to expire, no defining moment when I came face to face with my own mortality. No fanfare of choir voices came to accompany me to the Great Beyond. I simply floated out of the body and rose upward like a balloon, observing the scene below with detached fascination from a corner just a foot or two below the ceiling, while the medical team worked on the body.

Notice that I said 'the' body instead of 'my' body because the lifeless shell on the gurney with a sheet over its head wasn't me anymore. The *me* that is Judith McBride was still very much alive and aware, encased now in another kind of body. Not flesh and bone, but something lighter and more whole. A dead ringer, you should pardon the expression, for the physical vessel my soul had just vacated.

My spirit body was as tangible to me as the earthly body had been, yet there were subtle differences I noticed right off. I felt more vital and energetic than I ever had on earth, alert to the slightest stimulus, like I'd just awakened from a thirty-one year nap. A deep tranquility banished any fears or uncertainties of the transition taking place.

Despite the rather odd circumstances surrounding my demise, I didn't feel angry or sad that I had died. Oh, a little annoyed, maybe. After all, nothing got my knickers in a twist more than the best-laid plans of mice, men, and Judith going astray. All through high school, Micaela had teased me about being a control freak; she would go to town with this scenario. Judith McBride, dying when she didn't plan on it? Unthinkable.

I took a moment to examine this etheric body of mine and check out the new and improved me. I liked what I found. I ran my hands over my hair, noticing a silky thickness I hadn't known before. This wasn't the turmeric chaff I used to have. I tilted a shiny auburn lock this way and that, marveling at the color and texture. This was the hair I'd always dreamed of having, much the way women with poker-straight hair get perms and dishwater blondes go sun-kissed. Gone was the accursed frizz I'd had to flat iron straight every morning of my life. I felt like Cinderella after the fairy godmother changed her rags into a ball gown.

My hands slid down the smooth skin of my abdomen to my thighs, where they froze. I brought my hand back up to my belly. For the first time in my life, I had a stomach so flat it was almost concave. I had never been much of a fashion maven, mind you, but it would have been nice to shop for anything that struck my fancy instead of ferreting out styles to drape over the small pot that made me look like

I'd swallowed a papaya, whole. There is a God, and he's a celestial plastic surgeon. I wondered if they had bikinis in heaven...

I turned to the nurses hovering near the mannequin-like corpse on the gurney. "Hey," I called to them. "What on earth happened?"

No answer.

I called a little louder. "Hel-LO-O! Hey! Over here! What went wrong?"

No one looked up, and it finally dawned on me that they couldn't hear my voice. I heard them keenly, even though they spoke in hushed tones. I could even hear the staff in the next unit, and the receptionist down the hall.

A nurse went out to the waiting room to tell Micaela that Dr. Kreske wanted to speak with her. Micaela Pressman and I had been best friends since the seventh grade. She was everything I never was: a blue-eyed blonde who had never needed braces or control-top pantyhose. In high school she had been popular with everyone from the artsy drama kids to the cheerleaders. Her academic achievements landed her a spot at Brown University where she drove her male colleagues mad when she studied in the sunny quad wearing a Brazilian bikini. Micaela believed in multi-tasking: no reason why you couldn't get a tan while reading *Fundamentals of Microbiology.*

Our relationship spanned decades, longer than many of our friends' marriages. There were things Mic knew about me that no one else did, not even Saul. We were truly a bonded pair. Now she had the unenviable chore of breaking the news of my death to Saul. Poor Micaela. There's nobody on whom I'd wish this burden, but I hated that it had to be Mic. We hadn't bargained for this when we'd exchanged friendship necklaces in eighth grade. The silver pendant was half a heart with a zigzag edge as if it had been broken in two. Each half fit the other to recreate the whole heart. By these tokens we pledged unending sisterhood, come what may. At the time, we were thinking along the lines of major zit outbreaks and unrequited crushes, not untimely death and notification of next of kin.

My next of kin and I had often dreamed about someday buying a really big Airstream and touring the country at will. Now it looked like my immediate travel plans were limited to this near-earth location where newly-departed souls adjust to the afterlife. But how was I supposed to get around? Fly?

I shrugged and put one foot in front of the other, just like on earth. It worked. I moved as though on a mechanical sidewalk through an empty white corridor that looked like a spanking new hospital before any equipment was moved in. I wished someone was around to answer all my questions, but I seemed to be all alone. I blinked at the light glaring at the end of the corridor and kept walking. I had no idea where I was going; I just kept moving.

In short order I found myself inside a basement room at Goldblatt & Sons Funeral Home, morticians of choice for upscale Jews, the Fendi of formaldehyde. Lou Goldblatt, Jr.

was just putting the finishing touches to my earthly toilette, while Johnny Mathis crooned from the ancient console radio in the corner. Lou was short, fat, and bald, hardly the sort of person you want doing your makeup. But let's face it, he wasn't Monsieur Louis, Beautician to the Stars. He was sweaty Lou, costumer of the dead.

Handiwork complete, he stepped away from the table and we both got a good look at the finished product. The makeup gave new meaning to the term 'matte finish,' but the hair was the real problem. I looked like a flapper who'd danced one too many Charlestons. I guess Lou's wife Myrna hadn't bothered to look at the photograph Saul had provided. The wallet-size snap lay atop a scrambled sheaf papers on the dusty Formica desk behind the worktable. She had fashioned a coif that only stick-straight hair could carry off, certainly not my coarse mop. The result looked like Buckwheat meets Betty Boop. I flinched at the spit curls on my cheeks, longing to brush out all that Dippity-Doo and restore some semblance of me. What had Myrna been thinking?

I gave Saul props for his choice of burial outfits: a five-year-old Evan Picone suit, powder blue and taupe houndstooth checks with a blue and taupe shell in a coordinating pattern. He knew it was one of my favorites, even though for the past few years the skirt had been tight around the waist and pulled slightly across the derriere. Guess I wouldn't have to worry about the ill-fitting skirt anymore. Lou left the back zipper open and even ripped the seam a little to give the front of the skirt a smoother appearance. In fact, the outfit had never looked better on me.

A distant blaze of light flared once, beckoning me. I hadn't gone more than a few steps when I found myself in a field of headstones with small rocks placed on top. Some had many rocks heaped up in a pyramid; others had only a handful neatly arranged in a row on top of the granite.

A cluster of people encircled an open grave. Muffled crying provided backup for a familiar voice that rang in clear tones.

Micaela read something from a book that lay open in her hands. I glanced from her to the plain wooden coffin with a simple Star of David affixed to the lid. The scent of new pine struck my nostrils with a clarity that took me back to summer camp in the woods of Maine.

The surreal scene looked like a stranger's funeral instead of my own. My mother's chin wobbled and Micaela's voice quavered as she recited the beautiful passage from Wordsworth's *Ode on the Intimations of Immortality from Recollections of Early Childhood*. It was one of our favorite poems. *...though nothing can bring back the hour of splendor in the grass, of glory in the flower; we will grieve not...*

Micaela finished the verse and folded the book closed, cuing Rabbi Kalman to begin the mourner's *Kaddish*. With each intonation, a sublime rush infused my body, spreading to the tips of my toes and fingers, a rush that far eclipsed the giddy pleasure of being voted Fraternity Sweetheart two years in a row, the euphoria of helping a paralyzed patient walk again, or the dreamy elation of my wedding day. I became an ethereal sponge, soaking up love until I thought I could hold no more. If everyone on earth could know that each prayer, no matter how simple, really does reach departed souls and help in their transition to the other side, more people would pray oftener and with greater feeling.

Saul took up a garden shovel and scooped a small mound of loose dirt that he tossed onto the casket partially lowered into the grave. As he handed the shovel to Micaela, the sun's rays bounced off wet paths on their cheeks. The scene almost had *me* crying.

The graveside service concluded and the crowd dispersed to their cars. I followed them back my mother's house, where there was more food laid out than I'd seen since last Thanksgiving. Food in mass quantities is *de rigueur* on Jewish occasions, a kind of go-with-everything accessory suitable for mourning or celebrating. Mom had ordered some deli platters, but relatives, friends of relatives, and relatives of friends also brought over briskets and roast chickens and desserts. Grieving works up a big appetite. My mouth watered as Micaela placed a cheesecake on the dining room table. I no longer needed to eat, but the sensory pleasure of it wasn't diminished by death. Happily, such delights are only enhanced in the afterlife. I'd have missed the aroma of fresh-brewed coffee in the morning, the taste of chocolate-chip ice cream, the feel of a cashmere sweater against my skin.

People I hadn't seen in decades had come out of the woodwork, murmuring platitudes to Saul. *I know how you feel...it's God's will...at least she went quickly...now she can watch over you....* Poor Saul looked stricken, more so than at the cemetery. This open display of emotion was a rarity for my strong-but-silent man. Saul didn't always express his love in conventional ways, but I knew it was there. Now I felt his love at its purest, magnified a hundredfold. In death I didn't have to regret leaving loved ones behind. I took their love with me; the rest is insignificant.

Saul's sister Jessica stood by the dining room table with our accountant, a statuesque blonde named Mary Lynn Walker. There were two constants about Mary Lynn. One, she was forever correcting people who called her 'Marilyn.' Two, she always managed to find us sizeable tax deductions. I liked her, despite her drop-dead good looks.

Jessica was a different story. As pretty and innocuous as an angelfish, inside she was all shark. Five years older than her brother and with a personality that came on strong, she had always tried to bend Saul to her will. She never asked, she decreed. The word 'please' did not exist in her vocabulary, but somehow she got away with it. Accustomed to people doing as she told them, Jessica resented the fact that she never could manipulate me in the same way. We maintained an unspoken truce for Saul's sake, but our mutual dislike was undeniable. Saul was as blind to his sister's true colors as he had been to my too-tight Evan Picone skirt. I knew that, and Jessica knew that I knew it. This enabled her to exploit his ignorance at my expense.

"So awful about Judith," Mary Lynn tsk-tsked.

"Yes, Saul's taking it very hard, though what he ever saw in her... I told him I'd take care of her clothes. It's not healthy for him to hang on to them. The sooner they're gone, the sooner he can get on with his life."

Mary Lynn flashed a Cheshire smile. "Why, Jessica, that's so thoughtful of you."

"I just happen to wear the same size as Judith, not that I'll find much in her wardrobe worth keeping." Jessica gave a resigned sigh. "I tried for years to teach her how to dress, but she rarely took my advice. Even when she did, she never could develop any real sense of style."

Mary Lynn glanced across the room at the unmerry widower. "Poor Saul looks like a lost puppy. I'll see if he wants to come over for dinner next week. He'll need to get out of the house and be with close friends."

A strange heaviness in my lower body stole my attention from the conversation. I looked down at my stomach, but it was unchanged: smooth and flat. Nothing about my spiritual body appeared different from a moment ago, yet now I felt as though I was trying to swim to the surface in a waterlogged snowsuit, kicking and kicking but still dragged down. The grey mist swirling around me had become dense and thick with negativity from these two people pretending to mourn my tragic passing.

I bailed on the rest of *shiva* week, more than ready to move on to whatever awaited me in the spirit world. In retrospect, overhearing Mary Lynn and Jessica might have been the best way–the only way–to propel me forward to the next level of afterlife.

Don't misunderstand me; I wasn't completely cavalier about my own death. I may have accepted the reality of it with good grace, but the idea didn't thrill me to pieces. I had a pretty nice life on earth: great friends, a fulfilling career, and a husband who never left the seat up. Chunky thighs notwithstanding, I still wore a size eight. All in all, I didn't have much to complain about.

But here I was, so I might as well make the best of it and get on with this dance known as life after death. Before I left, though, I wanted to say goodbye to Saul.

I found him alone in the bedroom of our house. I looked around as an objective observer instead of a recent occupant. Everything looked the same: muted cappuccino walls and carpet, room dominated by the clean, spare lines of the Scandinavian furniture Saul didn't like at first but came to appreciate. He sat on the edge of the king-size bed, patting our Rottweiler, Max. Ginger the mutt lay on my side of the bed with her head on the pillow where the last vestige of my scent remained. Was it my imagination, or did she look sad? Ginger had very expressive eyes that spoke volumes. I always knew what she tried to say to me.

Saul, on the other hand, never spoke volumes with his eyes or anything else. Even in his solitude, his eyes were dry. I didn't need tears to tell me what I already knew. He was as devastated to lose me as I would have been to lose him. I yearned to reach out and stroke his hair, tell him everything would be okay, but I could only touch him from now on in ways he may not understand. When a spring breeze brushes his cheek, it will really be my caress he feels. When he smiles at the framed wedding photo on the bureau, it will be my embrace that puts the smile there. He won't know it's me, but someday he will find out. He will just have to do it in his own time.

Of its own accord, my arm reached down to him. I cupped his chin in my hand, feeling the fine stubble that never waited until five o'clock to shadow his face. He reached up and brushed his neck with his hand as if to swat away a pesky gnat. His hand slid behind his neck to massage the knotty muscles. I took my own hand and placed it over his, sending soothing thoughts of love and peace to blend with his own strokes.

With a final sigh, he slapped his palms on the top of his thighs as if he'd indulged in self-pity long enough. He crossed to the door and paused there, looking around the room as though he would never see it again. His eyes fell on the framed picture of me in my wedding gown that stood at one corner of the dresser. He ran a finger along the top of the frame, like he was inspecting for dust. I knew it was the caress he wasn't able to give me.

The door closed behind him before I realized my hand still stretched out in his direction. I was the one who wouldn't see it again. Not the way the room had been, full of the four earthly souls that occupied it. The life we knew together was over.

For now, anyway.

Chapter Two

I was never what they used to call 'date bait'. In fact, I had pushed the envelope of adolescent awkwardness to new lows. Even now, the memories are painful enough that I will omit the ugly specifics. Suffice it to say that I didn't have my first date until freshman year at NYU, and even that had been a blind date arranged through friends of my parents with their pimply son.

In college I finally exited my protracted 'awkward phase', but things in the romance department remained as dull as ever. I whined on the phone to Micaela, in Providence, about my dearth of dates.

"Good things come to those who wait," she counseled. "The right person will recognize your sterling qualities." I had my doubts, but Micaela's motherly platitudes lightened me up about the whole thing. She had a knack for showing me how to laugh at myself.

Senior year took a turn for the better one day at Healthy, Wealthy, & Wise, a fast-health-food place near the urban campus that catered as much to the student body as to the myriad law firms in the area. Soft-serve frozen yogurt was just emerging as the new trend in lunch-on-the-run for executives in power ties and secretaries in suits and Nikes.

Tables were always at a premium during the lunchtime peak between noon and one-thirty. I stood clutching my tray, scouring the crowded restaurant for an empty spot. For once, I was in the right place at the right time and snagged a table just as two lawyers were vacating. Their animated discussion was liberally sprinkled with terms like *discovery* and *deuces tecum*, and I'd spent enough lunch hours here to gain a working knowledge of attorney-speak.

I gloated over this serendipitous find and sat down to unload my tray. Just as I stoked a well-laden spoonful of chocolate-vanilla swirl yogurt with granola and wet walnuts into my mouth, a tall, skinny guy asked if he could share my table.

"There isn't another seat available," he apologized.

"Oorff, eezhs mmp," I invited as graciously as I could with a mouthful of yogurt.

He sat down while my reddened face returned to normal. Peering at the contents of my tray, he asked, "What have you got there on your yogurt?"

I hurriedly swallowed and croaked, "Wet walnuts."

"And granola." He calmly flicked a piece off his sleeve spewed forth by my reply.

I laughed, discomfort dissolved. How can you possibly remain uptight when you spit food on a perfect stranger? And, worse still, he comments on it? I lowered my eyes and looked at him through my lashes. The knot in his solid navy tie was loose and his white shirt was full of wrinkles. He displayed an awkwardness I thought kind of cute.

I found myself wondering if he found me attractive, but quickly banished the thought from my mind. I didn't want to spend an otherwise relaxing lunch hour trying to be personable and entertaining. Once I decided not to view my tablemate with romantic interest, I could talk easily with him. I even ordered a second yogurt, not caring what he thought.

At the end of lunch it was see you around, nice talking to you. By the end of the week we had shared a table twice more and I learned a little about Saul McBride. He turned out to be a Member of the Tribe in spite of the name McBride, which had been changed from Mandelberg by his anxious-to-assimilate grandfather. Why he didn't just shorten it to Mandel or even something ambiguous like Miller, no one knows. Maybe he took a wrong turn at Ellis Island and ended up in South Boston instead of New York's lower east side.

Saul was twenty-five and a public relations consultant. He asked what I did for a living and appeared surprised to hear that I was still in college. He said I seemed more mature.

I considered this and decided I liked it. *Mature*. Rarely had I heard a comment like that from my peers. Geeky, maybe. Certainly naive and sheltered. But nobody had ever called me mature. Then again, perhaps it wasn't so much what was said as who had said it. Over subsequent frozen yogurts with Saul, it occurred to me that maybe my lackluster love life had been the result of nothing more than having been around the wrong people. I said as much to Micaela on the phone.

"I won't say I told you so," she sang.

"Thank you."

"But I told you so."

"Cute, Micaela."

"Maybe he's the one."

"The one what?"

"The one I said would appreciate you. I bet you'll end up marrying this guy."

"Come on, Mic, we just met!"

"I can tell from your voice. This guy is special."

I blushed, glad that Micaela couldn't see. Saul *was* special. He accepted me for who I was. Not only did he accept me, he really seemed to like what he got.

Being with Saul proved to be my emancipation. He didn't deride my preference for ballet instead of bong parties. While most of the other kids at school celebrated TGIF at the campus pub, I was at the library on Friday afternoons to get my weekend studying out of the way. He thought I was very practical.

The anti-Harrison Ford with whom I had shared my lunch table became the boyfriend I initially disqualified. When we went to bed for the first time, I found out that Saul wasn't turned off by my papaya-gourd belly. He planted a kiss on my elevated navel and said that potbellies are considered very sensual in Middle Eastern cultures.

This guy was a keeper.

By the time he gave me an engagement ring for graduation, I noticed a definite softening to the acerbic wit that had been my armor against a world in which I didn't fit. Belonging to Saul gave me a heady feeling of self-worth, and I came to believe in those qualities he and Micaela had always seen. My parents threw us a big wedding that was more lavish than I would have planned myself, but my mother was so happy I didn't have the heart to tell her that it wasn't really my taste. I was an only child; she couldn't help herself. It wasn't easy to bite my tongue, but I went along with garden hats for the bridesmaids. I drew the line, however, at her plans for two wedding gowns, one for the ceremony and a different one for the reception. But I was most proud of my self-control when she'd say for the umpteenth time, "I never thought we'd see this day!" *Thanks, Ma.*

The early years of our marriage required the usual adjustment to any give-and-take partnership, but Saul and I were content. One thing we agreed on was the subject of kids. We didn't want any. Parenthood was a serious responsibility and I feared I'd screw it up. I had enough issues of my own; I didn't want to pass them on to the next generation. Saul didn't care either way, despite pressure from his father.

"How can you deny me grandchildren?" he lamented.

"I think Jessica has made up the deficit pretty well with the four you already have," I said.

"Four Katzes. There won't be a McBride left when I'm

gone. Who will carry on the family name, I ask you?"

"Family name? It isn't even ours," Saul pointed out. "Grandpa Izzy changed it at Ellis Island."

"Yes, well...your grandfather was afraid of sounding too Jewish. But McBride has been the family name for three generations now."

Saul and I looked at each other.

"I'll tell you what," he said to his father. "The day you change the family name back to Mandelberg, you let me know. Then we'll talk grandchildren."

And that, I thought, takes care of that.

I blossomed in many ways over the course of our eight-year marriage. Not only had I found true love, but life as a whole took on new meaning. At Saul's encouragement, I applied to graduate school and got a master's degree in physical therapy. He couldn't have been prouder or more supportive.

His own career flourished during this time. He landed a consulting position at a large PR firm that came with a hefty pay raise. But the money was of little consequence. Saul's father had made a fortune raising laboratory mice, an enterprise that didn't exactly earn this animal lover's seal of approval. I was glad when he sold the business to a pharmaceutical manufacturer, relieved of the burden of torn loyalty between my husband's family and my own principles. The sale brought millions, which Saul and Jessica stood to inherit. My father-in-law gave his two children sums of money just shy of the amount subject to the gift tax, saying he didn't want the government to get it all in taxes when he died. Though we appreciated the financial security, we vowed that our lifestyle would remain grounded. We had seen what happens to many *nouveau riche* and swore that money would not become our god.

Saul's new job put him on the road a good deal, but I didn't really mind. Much as I missed him, his absence afforded me time to indulge in a private passion (my confidence hadn't risen in all areas). I was shy about revealing that I dabbled in poetry, even to Saul. I was hardly any good, but enjoyed a certain satisfaction in putting down words and moving them around like chess pieces until they harmonized just right. I kept the poems in a spiral notebook that lived in isolation in the bottom drawer of my nightstand.

For a long, lovely while, the two of us had it all. Now Saul was a widower getting back to the business of living. I hoped he would start getting out a little. I wanted more for him than just Monday Night Football and solitary breakfasts at the IHOP with the morning paper. He deserved to experience the fullness of life, not just go through the motions of existing.

As they say, be careful what you wish for.

Chapter Three

"Welcome home."

I jumped and spun around, coming face to face with a tall, reedy man I didn't know. He smiled at me with the whitest teeth I'd seen this side of Hollywood. The smooth skin that stretched over high cheekbones made it impossible to guess if he was twenty-five or fifty. His mocha complexion gleamed in dark contrast to the long white caftan he wore. A tightly woven white skullcap perched like a pillbox on his close-cropped head.

The longer I looked at him, the more I believed he wasn't a stranger, that I should know this Nubian Ultra-Brite model. At that instant, a surge of energy passed through me like an electric current, exactly like the one I experienced while attending my funeral.

My eyes widened and I clamped a hand on my midsection. "Oh," came out like a hiccup.

The stranger chuckled. "Someone has just said *Kaddish* for you again," he explained in a lilting baritone with a trace of accent I couldn't identify. "Do not distress yourself. At first it is quite common to be startled by the prayer surge. Recently-released spirits are not quite accustomed to such abundant helpings of love." His formal speech seemed from another century.

He pressed his palms together lightly and made a shallow bow. "I am Ashraf, your spirit guide. I know you have many questions, and I am here to answer them for you...and to help you find your own answers."

"At the risk of sounding trite, where am I?"

We were inside a massive edifice as vast as an abbey. How I got there baffled me. One moment I was alone with Saul in my earthly bedroom; the next I stood in this strange building. Liquid sunlight seeped into every corner, conforming to the building's shape. I had no idea how the light penetrated it; there were no windows. The milky walls shimmered like a million opals, a fragment of light now and then catching a spark of hidden orange or violet and creeping like a slow flame along the marble surface.

The Pearly Gates?

I squatted down to examine the floor, shiny-cold and laid out in a single huge slab with no visible seams. I teetered on the balls of my feet and steadied myself with a hand on either side. I expected to feel an unyielding marble floor. Instead, my fingers met a warm, cushioned surface with a plush-carpet resiliency.

Ashraf smiled at my childlike exploration. He gestured toward the far end of the hall. "Let us walk and talk outside."

He paused by the portal, allowing me to pass through first. I stepped onto a landing and my breath caught in my throat at the beautiful scene outside. Velvety grass as lush as the Scottish moors spread as far as the eye could see, dotted with pristine gardens. Flowers of a hundred varieties bloomed in riotous color, more intense than the colors we see on earth. As a breeze with the spicy aroma of poppies wafted over my face, I thought this had to be the original Garden of Eden...or at least where all world-class gardeners go when they die.

Ashraf touched my elbow, breaking the hypnotic spell. He guided me down the steps to a stone bench under the shade of an almond tree. People strolled about in pairs and trios, deep in hushed conversations.

Ashraf noticed me noticing, and nodded toward them. "They are also spirit guides, helping other newly arrived souls become acclimated to their new environment." He spread his arms wide in presentation. "This is known as the astral plane, Judith, a kind of welcome center for spirit orientation." He regarded me closely. "I was somewhat concerned that you had tarried too long in the etheric realm immediately after your passing, but I can see now that you are transitioning well."

I blushed and averted my eyes. Ashraf covered my hand with his. "Do not feel embarrassed. You are not the first soul to have found closure by attending her own funeral. Very often a spirit does not accept the reality of her death until someone or something confirms it."

I wanted to dismiss the episode as a momentary lapse in judgment. "You probably think I'm petty and egotistical, wanting to hear people sing my praises." The words came out sounding more defiant than nonchalant.

"I am not here to judge you, Judith. None of us are. The love we have for you in the spirit world is unconditional. At this point in your development, the only one who can judge you is you."

I did feel love emanating from this curious soul who declared himself my spirit guide, as absolute as my parents' love for me, as deep as Saul's, as steadfast as Micaela's. Instinct told me that I could trust him, that I could safely lower the walls I had unwittingly put up.

In the space of seconds it took me to digest this revelation, Ashraf intuited my acceptance. "You will find the astral realm identical in every respect to the physical world you just left. This is where you will undergo the next phase of your adjustment to the spirit world."

"The next phase?"

"The rudiments of spiritual existence: transportation, communication, your goals for soul growth."

"But how is this place different from where I was right after I died?"

He used the same patient tone one might when explaining to a young child where babies come from. "There you existed one step beyond the physical world."

That made sense. "I seemed to be hovering above everything."

Ashraf nodded. "Here you will be in a dimension unto itself. You will interact with others, much as you did on earth, but in a spiritual environment instead of a physical one."

"But if this astral plane seems no different from life on earth, then what's so special about it? Seems to me that heaven should be...well, heavenly."

"That you shall learn for yourself, my dear. I cannot do the work for you. One does not transform instantaneously from fallible human into spiritual perfection. It is achieved over many lifetimes."

On the subject of reincarnation, I wasn't sure where I stood. I never quite believed in it, but I didn't disbelieve it, either.

"I am proud of your soul progression, Judith, particularly in the last several lifetimes," Ashraf continued.

The last several? "How many have I had?"

"Forty-nine."

That got my attention. Forty-nine lifetimes...the very thought wearied me.

My spirit guide stood up and ambled down the path, the pace of his feet matching his careful explanation. He didn't have to ask me to follow; I was a rat to his Pied Piper. "Soul progression is achieved through reincarnation and the lessons one learns during that incarnation. Some souls need only a few lifetimes; others need many more."

"How many have you had?"

"I chose to work on my spiritual growth while remaining here in the astral world. It is another option for soul development, but it takes longer to achieve."

"But why would you choose the longer road? Wouldn't

you rather speed up the process?"

"My choices are my own, Judith, as are the reasons behind them. We can only do what is right for ourselves."

I took the hint. "How long have you been my spirit guide?"

"Always," Ashraf replied. "I even helped foster your penchant for poetry."

"What did you have to do with my poetry?"

"Remember when you would struggle with a verse, knowing what you wanted to express but unable to release the proper words?"

"Do I. More often than I care to remember."

"Then there were times when the poems flowed without effort. Your fingers could not keep pace with your thoughts."

I nodded, eyes wide.

"That was I giving you a gentle push. Your creativity was bottled up, unable to flow freely. You just needed someone to uncork the bottle."

Ashraf's keen sensitivity caught the dejection on my face. "Celestial guidance does not relegate you to mediocrity, Judith." He bent his head to look me in the eye, compelling me to do the same. "Do you know that all the great masters of creativity through the ages received spiritual help? Shakespeare, Rembrandt, Beethoven, Balanchine...nobody does it alone. Some souls are more receptive to it than others."

I brightened a little at this. Even genius needs a little

help.

On impulse I asked, "May I call you 'Ash'?"

My spirit guide took both my hands in his. "Judith, my dear, to put it as you yourself would, you may call me anything you wish. As long as you call me."

For the rest of the afternoon, Ash filled me in on the fundamentals of the spirit world. He was the teacher, I was the student, and the course was Afterlife 101. He urged me not to feel overwhelmed, that I had all the time in the universe to absorb everything.

"There is no pressure here," he said. "You will not be given a written examination. You will find the spiritual realm a much kinder, gentler place than the earthly world you recently departed."

I smiled at his choice of words. "You know, President George Bush once used that very expression."

Ash got a positively devilish gleam in his eye. "Where do you think he got the idea?"

Chapter Four

After the experience with Jessica and Mary Lynn at my mother's house, you would think I'd have had my fill of eavesdropping.

Guess again.

Despite my determination not to hang onto my earthly life, I still worried about Saul. It couldn't hurt to check in to see how he was doing. Ashraf had told me that celestial transportation is really nothing more than teleportation. "Every soul, embodied or not, emits energy vibrations. Souls in the afterlife just do so at a faster rate than people on earth."

"That would make a great bumper sticker. *Old spirits never die; they just vibrate faster.*"

"Bumper sticker?"

"Yes, it's a–never mind."

He showed me how to close my eyes and focus all my thoughts and energies on my destination, then take a step. When I opened my eyes, I would be there. He started me off on small trips, always with him at my side like a parent who steadies his child on a two-wheeler for the first time. The hardest part was taking that first step. I felt as though I was going to fall.

"Why am I so hesitant to take a simple step?" I asked him.

"It is only because this mode of transportation is a new experience for you. Do not worry; it will not last. Trust yourself."

Soon it seemed as if I'd been riding the energy waves all my life. It became as natural as breathing.

This would be the first time I had seen Saul since the funeral, when he'd been as bereft and vulnerable as any self-respecting widower should. I expected to find him now in much the same condition.

Imagine my surprise at finding him dressed to the nines in tie and jacket, preening in front of our bedroom mirror. Max and Ginger perched on the bed watching him, panting slightly at their master's odd behavior. Saul wasn't one to dress up except when a special occasion demanded it. When it did, he grabbed a random tie from the rack and invariably paired it with a rust-colored sport coat older than I. Rarely did the selections coordinate. A few times I tried buying him some beautifully matched shirts and ties, but for some reason he never wore the sets together. My purchases always ended up being worn with the rust jacket, and the resulting ensemble was often comical. Like his patriotic phase when he wore his American flag tie with any random shirt, no matter the color or pattern. Partnered with the rust jacket, he sometimes resembled a TV test pattern.

I gave up eventually, but never understood his crazy attachment to the provincial rust number. He could be so stubborn sometimes.

Long ago I had resigned myself to letting Saul be Saul, but the man now standing before the mirror was someone else entirely. If the new clothes he wore didn't prove that, the thicket of hair covering his upper lip did. My Saul with a moustache? He had told me more than once that a youthful attempt at growing a moustache had sworn him off facial hair. He showed me a photo of himself at college graduation with a narrow strip of black under his nose that made him look like the Frito Bandito.

Maturity had apparently heightened Saul's hirsute inclinations, for he now sported a cookie duster worthy of Tom Selleck. He'd also been working out. His shoulders were more pronounced and he carried himself taller. I admired the way his blue jacket flattered his new physique, but why the sudden Mr. Universe aspirations?

He actually hummed as he futzed with the knot of his tie. No wonder Ginger and Max watched him so closely. They probably wondered who this strange man was, and what he had done with their master.

The doorbell rang. Saul gave himself a final appraisal in the mirror and all but skipped to the front door, the dogs in close pursuit. He opened it and leaned outward to the visitor, his hand still grasping the doorknob. Ginger and Max lost interest and retreated to the bedroom. I heard the sound of a female voice and lips smacking on lips.

"Hey there, handsome. You didn't need to get all duded up. We're only going to Gino's."

Saul, overdressed for a date at *our* favorite restaurant? And the lucky bachelorette is...?

Our accountant, Mary Lynn Walker.

Saul having dinner with her made sense; she probably handled my estate for him. Mary Lynn had always gone the extra mile for us. I laughed with relief, but quickly stifled the sound. Then I remembered they couldn't hear me, so I laughed aloud again, just because I could.

"I wish you had let me pick you up, M.L.," Saul said.

M.L.?

"I had to bring these over anyway." She shifted a stack of documents from one arm to the other. "Why should you make an extra trip?"

"Thoughtful as always." Saul took the papers from her. "Would you like a drink, or shall we just go on to the restaurant?"

"Why don't we have a drink here first? Our reservation isn't for another hour."

Saul carried the documents into the den and Mary Lynn headed for the bar cart. She mixed two scotch-and-waters and handed one to Saul as he came back in.

Saul hates scotch.

Throaty laughter floated through the air. Mary Lynn absently tossed errant blonde locks over her shoulder, the deliberate movement anything but casual. She was playing the sex kitten, playing it to the hilt. You would think someone named 'Mary Lynn' would be the wholesome, girl-next-door type, as good as bread, and just as spongy. Then you find out she's the complete antithesis of her name and all preconceived images fly out the window. After all, you don't look at Goldie Hawn and think of *bubbe* and matzo ball soup, right?

Mary Lynn may have spent most of her life correcting people who called her 'Marilyn,' but as far as I could tell, she wouldn't have to anymore. Tonight she lived up to the name 'Marilyn' and all it implied.

I took a good look at her for the first time since she entered the house. Her figure stood to full advantage in a black silk pants suit paired with a brief silk camisole. Strappy stiletto sandals showcased red-polished toenails that matched her perfectly manicured fingertips.

Acrylic overlays. Had to be. Mary Lynn Walker bites her nails.

With a predatory gleam in her eye that only another woman would catch, she moved closer to Saul and lightly brushed his moustache with her finger. "*Mmmm*, it's coming along nicely. I told you a moustache would make you look even sexier."

Saul kissed the fingertip tracing his lip. "I have that, and a few other things to thank you for," he murmured.

"Don't mention it," Mary Lynn purred. "What are accountants for?"

The kiss that followed was something I didn't really want to witness but couldn't tear myself away from. Simultaneous emotions ran through me—surprise, embarrassment, maybe even a little prurient curiosity—but I'm proud to say that true jealousy wasn't among them. Saul was a healthy, red-blooded male; I didn't expect him to turn monk in his widowhood...did I?

As for Mary Lynn, she was an intelligent, attractive woman with a dynamite figure. She was also a good friend and associate who had been close to us for years. It seemed only natural that Saul would feel comfortable with her. Who was I to begrudge him a little fun? Maybe she'd forget herself in the throes of passion and reveal some classified tax tips.

They were still kissing passionately when I rang down the curtain on that scene. It was one thing to wish Saul happiness; quite another to see the tangible evidence. I had an understanding nature, but masochistic I wasn't. Saul was my husband, my best friend besides Micaela. I wasn't immune to the effects of seeing Saul in the arms of another woman. She nuzzled his neck, but I was the one who breathed in the woodsy scent of his cologne. The memory was potent.

I had wanted Saul to go on living his life, didn't I? Now he was, with a little help from our accountant. I tried to be happy for him, but I had the gnawing feeling that he could be thinking with the wrong set of brains.

None of that, I chided myself. If Mary Lynn is–excuse me: 'M.L.'–is what makes Saul happy, then I'd learn to deal. This wasn't a competition and she wasn't my rival. This was about letting a loved one love again.

But if she's better in bed than me, I might have to pull out all her hair.

Chapter Five

Back in the astral plane, I tried to keep myself busy so my thoughts wouldn't wander back to Saul and Mary Lynn. Ashraf cautioned me not to become too comfortable here, though. "Remember that the Welcome Center is merely a springboard toward your permanent home. Very soon you will move on to the astral level suited to your present spiritual development."

"The ethereal level, the astral level–what's up with all that?" I whined. "This is supposed to be heaven, not a corporate structure."

"Up Here it is much like a ladder. Each rung is a realm of higher soul progression. As your soul evolves, you ascend another rung."

"What's at the very top?"

He looked at me sideways and grinned. "What do you think is at the very top?"

"God, of course. Who else?"

"Ah, who else, indeed. There is quite a–what is the expression–'Who's Who' on that topmost rung: Buddha, Moses, Jesus, Mohammed, Confucius…souls who have evolved to the highest level possible. God exists in all of us, Judith. We all have the same opportunity to reach the top of the ladder."

He raised a cautionary finger. "But know this. We may not simply clamber up whenever we are so inclined. We must work toward that elevation by learning, improving ourselves. Then we are obliged to come back down and teach others what we have learned."

It occurred to me that if earthly societies would only conduct themselves according to this system, how much better off the world would be. I indulged in a brief fantasy of Judith's Second Coming, saving the world through my sagacity. I shook my head to banish the vision before Ash had a chance to detect it. It wasn't always convenient having a spirit guide who could read your thoughts.

Ashraf's hand cupped my elbow. "Come, this way. We have one final matter to attend to before I dispatch you to your resident level."

Thank goodness he didn't mention my fantasy.

When coloring books were still my ultimate childhood pastime, I used to amuse myself with an activity called Black Magic. I took a blank piece of paper and filled it with a mosaic of crayon colors in random patterns. When I had every inch of the paper colored in, I covered the entire surface with a thick layer of black crayon. Then, with an empty fountain pen or an old ballpoint pen, I etched the outline of a picture. The rainbow of colors appeared through the black coat: Black Magic.

This is how heaven appeared on the glitter-strewn

beach where Ashraf brought me: a black velvet sky with stars reflecting the glitter. Or was the beach reflecting the glitter in the heavens, alive with shooting stars and meteors? The sky was a Black Magic background to the luminous show, yet warm yellow light cast elongated shadows on the sand, both sides of the clock blending together. It was the friendliest night I had ever seen.

At the far end of the beach, something was taking shape, blurry at first, then becoming clearer. A small white animal came running full-tilt toward me. The closer it came, the better I could make out a glossy white coat splotched with brown. The half-brown, half-white face looked just like my—

"Alexis," I shrieked in joyful disbelief, squatting down to greet the furry bundle that ran to me, full speed ahead. It *was* Alexis, the darling spaniel Saul and I had lost to Lyme disease when both dog and marriage were only two years old.

Alexis toppled me with thirty-five pounds of enthusiasm, and I gave myself over to the sandpapery tongue lapping my face. "Oh, Alexis," I kept saying over and over. When I finally opened my eyes—for some reason, Alexis liked to lick them—we'd been joined by another spirit, this one in human form.

"Hi, Judith. My name's Suse J. That's S-U-S-E, but pronounced *soo-zee*."

I took in the lean, lanky woman with light brown hair hanging just to her shoulders and straight, heavy eyebrows to match. She must have been over six feet tall. "What's the *J* for?" It came out as a sputter because Alexis took advantage of my open mouth to stick her tongue inside.

"Jehovah's Witness." She gave a quick laugh at some *double entendre* I didn't get. "Never mind. It doesn't stand for anything. It's just a middle initial with no period, like Harry S. Truman."

Her answer was no answer, but she dismissed the issue with a wave of her hand. "It's just a nickname I acquired long ago. Actually, I'm here only as a spokesperson, since your real Welcome Wagon–and I mean W-A-G-G-I-N–was designated as your official greeter. My regular assignment is receiving small children and babies who cross over by themselves."

A sudden chorus of happy barks coming from a cluster of mango trees, beyond the beach, interrupted her explanation. Two more dogs broke through the foliage and cantered toward us over the sand. Alexis' tail started wagging triple time. One of the dogs was a black Labrador Retriever I didn't recognize, but the other one I knew at once: Melly, the little mutt I had grown up with. Her real name was Melange, a name my mother came up with 'to reflect her mixed heritage,' but was inevitably shortened to Melly.

Melly touched noses with Alexis in greeting, but the other dog hung back politely while Melly and Alexis crawled all over me.

Suse J knelt down beside him to stroke his sleek coat.

"This is Midnight. His family isn't up Here yet, so I thought he might like to come along with us to help welcome you. Right, boy?" Midnight thumped his tail and licked Suse's nose.

I knelt and extended a hand to Midnight, who sniffed it with interest. "You all alone up Here, poochie?" I crooned, petting him. He leaned his full weight against me.

When I straightened, Suse J was smiling. "Welcome to level Seven, Judith. I know some animal spirits that will be very happy you've arrived."

I nodded, only half listening. I wasn't sure what Suse meant about the animal spirits, but it didn't really matter. I was learning fast. Up Here my questions seemed to answer themselves. Was it the change in environment, or was it I who was changing?

"Come on, let's get you settled," Suse J said. As we left the beach, canines prancing behind, she invited me to a reception at her own house here on level Seven.

"It's a weekly event for new arrivals, held at a different home each time," she explained. "Each level sponsors its own get-togethers."

I tried to imagine what kind of receptions might be held on the lowest levels. Probably not very festive.

Suse J said the spirit communities up Here are much like the residential neighborhoods I knew on earth. The best part is that homeowners' covenants up Here have nothing to do with the location of your swimming pool or the color you want to paint the exterior.

"The very soul which makes man a social animal in the physical world is no different on the other side. Spirits may not require shelter from the elements, but they still long for a slice of heaven they can call their own," she explained.

I spent the remainder of that first afternoon putting my place together. When I finished, I stood back and studied the effect: a combination of Barbie's Dream House and Mary Richards' Minneapolis apartment. I hadn't had this much fun since I redecorated Saul's condo right after we got engaged.

Suse J's reception that night reminded me of a real-estate open house. Spirits milled about her charming bungalow that looked like it belonged in a rural English village. I wouldn't have been surprised if Cotswold sheep had grazed nearby.

I searched for my hostess in the sea of people. She was easy to spot, towering above the heads in the crowd. She caught sight of me and waved. She excused herself from her companions and came over to greet me.

I returned her welcoming hug and asked, "Is Ashraf going to be here, too?"

"Ashraf had to attend a meeting of the Spirit Council tonight," she answered. "Otherwise he wouldn't miss your first reception. He sponsors several spirits on level Seven, you know, and can't be everywhere at once. He asked me to take special care of you tonight, but I told him you wouldn't need any hand-holding."

I wasn't sure if that was a compliment or not. "What

did Ash say to that?"

"Nothing. He just gave me one of his enigmatic looks."

"He does that to me all the time. It's nice to know I'm not the only one."

She led me through the crowd, making introductions all around. Everyone I met was as comfortable as well-worn jeans. They received me as an old friend who had been away on an extended trip and finally returned.

I mentioned this to Suse J, after everyone had departed and we sat alone in her kitchen, glad to get off our feet. "That's exactly what you are," she said. "This is home, Judith. The time we spend on earth is just temporary. You felt right at ease here tonight because you've known all these spirits before."

That explained why I repeatedly had a sense of *deja vu*, why the unknown also seemed familiar. My past and my present had finally caught up with each other, to be reenacted in my future.

Up Here, serenity is a superlative reward in itself, but there must also be a purpose to our existence. So spirits have jobs, just like people on earth. Of course, we don't have to worry about pension plans or dental coverage. We just find what we enjoy doing and go do it.

The job of tending to the souls of pets whose owners were still on earth belonged to an exuberant spirit named Denise. She was about to start what she hoped would be her final reincarnation and needed a replacement for her animal job. Suse J knew I'd be happy to oblige; that's why she made that remark on the beach. I couldn't imagine a nicer job than looking after peopleless pets.

Denise spent a few days introducing me to the pets in her care and showing me around the domain where they spent their time waiting for their humans to arrive. Dressed in red patent-leather mules and a zebra-striped micro mini, she was definitely one of a kind. She even described herself as the kind of blind date boys avoided at all costs. "When they heard 'short on looks but long on personality,' most of them ran in the other direction," she laughed.

It's a shame they never got past the exterior and gave her infectious personality a chance.

"What did you do in your last earthly life, Denise?" We lolled on the grass, soaking up the sun with some cats.

"I was a model."

I took in the bushy eyebrows and pitted skin and tried not to sound as incredulous as I felt. "A model?"

She chuckled. "Everyone has that reaction." She slid a foot out of the red mule and held it aloft, twisting it this way and that. "A foot model."

I looked at the perfect contour, unblemished skin, and French pedicure. Then I glanced down at my own feet in green rubber flip-flops. Staring back at me were two large bunions and several long hairs sprouting from my big toes.

She twitched her shoulders impishly. "To tell the truth, I get a kick out of messing with people that way, telling them I'm a model and watching them try not to act shocked."

I had to admire her impish sense of humor. She was content in her own skin and I envied that kind of confidence. It would serve her well in her next life.

"Suse J tells me you're dog crazy. Which ones are your favorites?"

"All of them! But there's something about the wild animals that show up now and then."

"Yeah, those babies are pretty hard to resist, aren't they?"

I nodded. "I think I hold a special place in my heart for them. Survival of the fittest is one thing, but to be picked off by a poacher just to become an ingredient in some primitive aphrodisiac is something else altogether."

Denise smiled. "Judith, you're just a sucker for a lost soul."

"Guess I am, but isn't that what it's all about? Looking out for each other? I mean, if all I cared about was taking care of Number One, I wouldn't be much of an evolved spirit."

Denise looked at me sidelong. "Careful, honey. You aren't at the top of the ladder yet."

"But there must be a reason why I was assigned to level Seven." My eyes grew wide. "I'll bet I'm supposed to be Saul's guardian angel!"

"Who's Saul?"

"My husband. He's a changed man since he started dating a friend of ours and I'm a little worried about him."

Denise rested her chin on her upraised knees and gave me a knowing glance. "Uh huh."

"No, really. You don't know him. He's acting like a teenager in love."

"And that's a problem because…?"

I didn't have a logical answer to that. "I'm just worried about my husband and want to watch over him. I care. Is that so strange?"

"Okay, okay. Just remember that you're not supposed to interfere with destiny."

"I won't. I just want to keep an eye on things."

Denise didn't look convinced, but she dropped the subject. We talked about the animal domain until she stood up and brushed the grass off her skirt.

I hugged her and wished her all the luck in the world with her new life. "Be careful out there."

"You too, Jude. You too."

"But I–"

Before I got any farther, she was gone. If there was something I had to be careful of, I wished she hadn't been so mysterious about it.

Chapter Six

Now that I had responsibilities up Here that I couldn't neglect, it was important that I not let my newfound dedication to Saul become all-consuming. At least level Seven spirituality granted me the understanding that concerned interest is one thing; obsession is another. Besides, knowledge is power. If I wanted to use otherworldly abilities to help Saul, I needed to learn exactly what they are and what limitations I would have. So the best thing I could do for both of us now was to arm myself with a greater understanding of life up Here.

I started by attending a lecture for newcomers given by none other than Suse J. She certainly played a variety of roles up Here: greeting newcomers, hosting receptions, assigning jobs. There had to be more to her than just the free-spirited Bohemian I saw, but I couldn't take the time right now to find out.

I discovered, though, that she was a great public speaker. In a gentle but compelling voice she explained how the spiritual world encompassed both heaven and hell.

"The common belief many people on earth have is that heaven exists in a lofty place high above us, with hell wallowing below."

Yeah, and I was one of them.

"Both heaven and hell are up Here, existing as different levels."

A ladder, just as Ashraf said.

Suddenly it all made sense. After all, life on earth is a series of rungs to climb; why should the afterlife be any different? Don't we all have to reach persistently for that higher rung to achieve our goals, fulfill our dreams?

Suse J went on talking, but I couldn't concentrate on anything she said. My brain started spinning out of control with this epiphany. Which was odd, because this wasn't the first time I heard it. Ashraf had also told me about the ladder, but it didn't have much impact until Suse J spoke the same words. I looked around at the other faces listening to her with rapt attention. She had them spellbound. We were a captivated, if not captive, audience.

I caught only bits and pieces of the rest of the lecture. When Suse J touched on spiritual transportation, I knew I should focus, but my mind kept whirring with questions. How could I help Saul and still improve my own spiritual growth? Are the two goals mutually exclusive, or will I be achieving one at the same time I'm doing the other?

Suse J wound up the lecture with questions from the audience. She pointed to a dark-haired man who raised his hand tentatively.

He spoke so softly, I had to strain to hear his question. "Can we visit other levels, just to see what they're like?"

Suse J's own brand of humor made an appearance. "A

very good question. And the answer is yes and no."

The poor spirit who had asked the question looked as though he wanted to disappear. His eyes went wide, his chin braced against his neck like a Marine Corps recruit.

Suse J eased up on him. "Visits to other levels are encouraged, but there's one catch. You can only visit levels below the one you're currently assigned. That means all of you can travel to the first six levels to your hearts' content, but Eight and Nine are off limits until you've earned a permanent promotion there."

My attention drifted again while Suse J made her closing remarks. I couldn't wait to see what the other levels were like, but where to go first. I was pretty sure I didn't want to start at the bottom. I didn't need Ashraf to tell me I wasn't ready for a visit to hell, no matter how brief.

A smattering of applause broke into my thoughts, and the hum of movement and low conversation spread with the departing crowd. I made my way out alone. I wanted time to think.

I set out to go exploring the next day. There was just one problem. I didn't know how to transport myself. I cursed my leapfrog brain for missing that part of the lecture. Well, I would go with my instincts and see what happens.

I shrugged my shoulders and closed my eyes, focusing on the general area below level Seven. *Wherever I land, that's where I'll explore.* I suppressed the urge to click my heels together and recite, "There's no place like home…there's no place like home…"

When I opened my eyes, it was clear I wasn't in Kansas anymore. The waxy-white sky was glaring, even though the sun didn't quite penetrate the persistent haze. The damp and oppressive atmosphere gave me a shuddery, claustrophobic feeling I didn't like. I looked down at the barren ground pockmarked by a few wilted flowers that didn't come close to the abundance and color on my own level.

I test-sniffed the air. There wasn't a hint of fragrance, but that didn't really come as a shock. From the look of the place, pleasing aromas probably weren't on the agenda. I spied an errant honeysuckle vine trailing out of a scraggly bush and bent toward it, hoping for that familiar heady scent. It had no smell at all. I plunged my nose deep into one of the sad blooms. Nothing.

Honeysuckle that didn't smell sweet? What was going on here?

I rubbed a dusty leaf between my fingers just to make sure it wasn't plastic. The plant was genuine, all right, but seemed more like an unreasonable facsimile.

I stood up, brushing dust from my hands. I still stood at the same spot where I had arrived, and at this rate I wouldn't get very far. I squinted at the horizon with my hand as a visor against the hazy glare. About half a mile away, I spied a cluster of ramshackle dwellings. It seemed as good a place to start as any. I began walking.

The closer I got, the clearer it became that the houses here were a country mile from the ones I knew on level Seven. Chipped and peeling paint, cinder blocks striped with mildew, window shutters falling away from their frames. The cracker-box structures were crowded together, which only added to my claustrophobia. On Seven, a dwelling is only as close to the next one as the occupants wish them to be.

I gave it the benefit of the doubt. Maybe this was just a particularly close-knit community.

I stopped at the first house I encountered. The concrete-block exterior had once been white, but long-term exposure to soot and grime had left it a dingy grey. The matchbook-size yard was a mess of turned-over dirt and coarse weeds.

"You want something?"

A disheveled man in worn, faded Levis and a black leather jacket stood outside the doorway, watching me. I tried to decide how old he was; he looked to be in that no-man's land between irrepressible youth and pragmatic adulthood. He might have been anywhere from eighteen to thirty. I guessed him to be in his late twenties.

"You want something?" he repeated, rubbing a hand back and forth over the dark patch of stubble shadowing his chin.

My stomach churned a little. He was no Saul McBride, that's for sure. The only remotely pleasant feature in his scruffy face were his piercing blue eyes. They glinted like beads in those deep-set sockets.

I shifted my weight from one foot to the other. What could I say? I was just browsing? I didn't want to make the guy feel like he was on display in a zoo.

"I'm, uh, visiting. From level Seven."

He gave a snort. "Felt like slumming, huh?"

O-kay. The natives weren't too friendly. Maybe someone else around here might be willing to share some information with me, someone with a little less attitude. Who needs this jerk? I started to walk away.

The Mickey Rourke wannabe followed me. "Hey, where you going?"

I ignored him and kept on walking.

"Hey, I'm sorry, okay? I figured you was from the high-rent district, coming to gloat over us poor, imperfect souls way beneath you."

I stopped and turned around. "High-rent district?"

"Yeah. Top of the ladder. Heaven Central. Where the big boys live."

While I deciphered these metaphors, he took a pack of Marlboros–unfiltered–from his jacket, smacked the bottom once against his palm, and pulled out a protruding cigarette with his lips. He fished a lighter from his other pocket, fired the cigarette, then held out the pack to me.

"No, thanks."

He shrugged and took a long drag, turning his head away before he exhaled in a surprising gesture of consideration. Smoke poured out of his nostrils and he became a fire-breathing dragon. I guess one spirit's distasteful earthly habit is another spirit's eternal pleasure.

"So. Who are you?"

"Judith McBride. And you?"

"Justin."

"Justin what?"

Another derisive snort. "You would ask that." The large chip on his shoulder supersized. "The name's Caso, if it's so fuckin' important."

What had I said that offended him so?

"My parents had a warped sense of humor," he added ruefully.

I got it then, and burst into laughter. *Just-in-case-o.*

Justin didn't share my amusement, but I couldn't really blame him. He'd probably been living down that name for a good many years.

He threw down the unfinished cigarette and ground it viciously into the dirt with the toe of his Doc Marten. He hunched his shoulders deeper into his jacket and headed back toward his front door. "Yeah, well, I'll see ya."

"Hey, wait," I called after him. "I didn't mean to insult you. Please don't go in yet."

He halted at the doorway and spun around to glower at me. "You're like all the rest. Just come down here to get a good laugh. Well, you got it now, so go somewheres else and leave me alone."

"No, it's not like that. Really. I'm not even sure where I am, but I certainly didn't come here to laugh at you. I like your name. I think your parents had a...creative sense of humor."

He looked out across the neighboring yards as if

pondering my sincerity. He ran a callused hand over his black D.A., thick with Brylcreem. I guess he decided I deserved a second chance because he sat down right there on a patch of crabgrass. He drew his knees up and rested his forearms on them, one hand clasping the other wrist. His eyes held a challenge when they looked up at me.

Did he want me to join him? Or did he wait for me to sit down just so he could have the pleasure of kicking me out? Unsure of what my next move should be, I did nothing.

"Whatsa matter? Afraid you'll spoil your pretty dress?"

I detested mind games like this, but saw no way around it. How else could I prove my good intentions? I sat myself down on the hard-packed dirt a foot or two away from him.

Justin lit another cigarette. "So. What level you on, Judith?" He had put me in my place; now he exaggerated the syllables of my name just to keep me there.

I squirmed, trying to find a comfortable position. Sitting on the ground gracefully in a dress is an exercise in futility. I lifted my hips and pulled out a twisted section of skirt from beneath me. "Uh, level Seven."

"Yeah? Must be nice."

His sarcasm was getting on my nerves. "It is nice, but it wasn't exactly handed to me on a silver platter, you know. I earned my place there."

"Okay, okay. Don't get all defensive on me. I just meant it has to be a sight better than this." Justin inclined his greasy head in the general direction of the other houses.

Another game. If I agree with him, I'm arrogant. Disagree, and I'm a patronizing liar.

"I don't know," I fumbled. "I mean, that's why I came down here, to see what other levels are like. Would you show me around a little?"

"Christ, lady, you made it up to level Seven and you wanna roam around down here?" He shook his head. "I don't get it."

I refused to answer. Either he would do it or he wouldn't, but I was through explaining myself.

Justin let out an exasperated sigh. "Come on, then, if you really want to." He tossed away the still-burning cigarette and leaped to his feet. He reached down for my hands to pull me to mine. Again I was taken aback by the incongruous chivalry. Maybe he wasn't the total hard-ass he wanted me to believe.

I remained silent as we walked past the other dilapidated houses in the settlement. He was quiet, too, but little by little, he let down his guard and began asking questions.

"So what did you in?" he queried.

Still embarrassed about my episode with the laxative granules, I chose my words carefully. "Fatal reaction to some drugs." No need to go into the gory details.

"No shit, you did drugs? You don't seem the type. Coke, I bet. Your kind always goes in for blow."

My kind? "Not recreational drugs, prescription medication."

"Sure. And I'll bet you told the sleazy doc who gave it to you that you had 'unbearable migraines.'"

I let that one slide. "It was during an endoscopy."

He gave a long whistle. "That's a ten-dollar word. I'm not even gonna ask what it means."

"It's a type of medical exam." I hoped he wouldn't ask what for.

"How'd your family make out in the lawsuit?"

Relieved that we headed away from touchy territory, my voice almost sang. "Oh, they didn't sue. I wouldn't have wanted them to."

"Are you messed up? They coulda made a nice deal with the hospital, gotten something good outta something shitty. What's with you people?"

My kind. You people. The judgmental references rankled, but we were talking so easily with each other that I didn't want to lose ground by arguing with him. He was my tour guide, my link to realms unknown. And anyway, something told me it would be pointless to show him the error of his ways. It usually was with people like him. So I changed the subject instead.

"How did you die, Justin?"

"Car accident."

I grimaced. "Who was drinking, you or the other driver?"

Justin halted in his tracks and narrowed his eyes at me. "You're so sure it was drunk driving. You know it all, don't you?"

"I just assumed—"

"You assumed. You assumed wrong. You sure ain't learned much being dead, Ms. J. The last thing someone from your neck of the woods should do is jump to conclusions."

"Wait a minute; you're lecturing *me* on prejudgment?"

"It just so happens nobody was drinking," he went on, as if I hadn't said anything. It really pissed me off to be dismissed like that. "I had narcolepsy."

Anger dissolved into curiosity. "I've heard of that. Isn't that when you unexpectedly fall asleep?"

"Bingo. I fell asleep at the wheel and plowed into a telephone pole. Car crumpled up like an accordion."

"Oh my God, Justin, I'm so sorry."

"You and me both."

"Frankly, I'm surprised they would even issue a driver's license to a narcoleptic."

"They wouldn't. But that didn't stop me from driving. Always drove by the book so I wouldn't get pulled over. Never went over the speed limit, never even changed lanes without a fuckin' turn signal. I was the best driver on the road...'til I wrecked, anyway."

There was something piteous behind his glib words. I felt a little sorry for him. "Not a pretty way to go."

"Not pretty, but no real biggie. I was outta the physical body before I even felt anything. That's S.O.P. in sudden or violent deaths like mine." As he uttered the last few words, his voice held the faintest quaver.

For all his bravado, Justin exuded a vulnerable quality I found endearing. It brought back memories of Saul, clumsy and wrinkled, the little flaws I first fell in love with. I had to admit it was nice to be with someone else who had residual earthly faults. With Justin, I didn't have the little needles of inferiority that sometimes pricked me around Ashraf or Suse J.

I put a hand on his shoulder. "I'm sorry if I sounded pompous before."

He kicked at a small stone. "Ah, what the hell. Guess I asked for it. Anyway, it was a lesson I had to learn in that life. 'Karmic debt,' they call it."

"What lesson?"

"Trying to control things outta my control. Thinking I could beat the narcolepsy and the system all at the same time. All it got me was a totaled T-bird and a one-way ticket up Here."

"Not one-way, Justin. You can go back to earth and try again."

"Yeah, but I figure maybe I was meant to learn the hard way. I'm gonna stay up Here to work on my soul. It may take longer, but at least I know I'll be doing it the right way. The forever way."

Justin came off like a ruffian, but he knew what he wanted and where he was going, which was more than I could say. To have the kind of insight to work on his soul the long way...there was more to Justin Caso than met the eye. Especially since he ended up Here on–

"Justin, what level is this?"

"You're on level Four, sweetness. Take a good look around. Aren't you glad you didn't end up here?"

The extent of his bitterness surprised me. True, level Four was nothing like Seven, but it wasn't as bad as he would have me think. The lower levels had to be much worse. Still, I guess it is all relative.

I decided I'd explored enough for one trip. Tonight was my turn to host a newcomers' reception and I had to get the house ready. To spare myself Justin's inevitable ridicule, I didn't tell him why I had to go home. But I did ask him if I could come back sometime to continue the tour.

"Sure, Ms. J., sure." He spoke somewhat affably through lips clamped on the ever-present cigarette. "I ain't going nowheres."

The last thing I saw before closing my eyes to transport myself home was his farewell hand held up like a stop sign. It was as eloquent a gesture as I would ever get from him.

I hurried home to set up for the reception. Eating is purely for aesthetic pleasure up Here, but cooking had been one of my earthly pleasures so I looked forward to preparing for this party. I'm a pretty good cook, too. Ripe brie baked in puff pastry, Portobello mushroom caps stuffed with spinach and crabmeat, assorted miniature quiches...

As I got busy in my light-filled kitchen, I thought about Justin Caso. What would he have to say about tonight's gathering? Would his predictable put-down stem from contempt for 'my kind,' or would it be just sour grapes from a downtrodden soul who still had a few life lessons to learn?

Meeting him made me even more curious about level Four and below. Ash had said we all are obligated to return and teach others what we have learned...maybe I could help some of the souls below, souls like Justin. I could mentor him in his spiritual growth, help him accelerate the process a little. It was the perfect way to make sure my concern for Saul didn't eclipse my other spiritual duties.

The doorbell announced the arrival of the first guests. Before I gave myself over to the gaiety of the party, I tucked away a few of the quiches. I would take them to Justin next time I visited.

Chapter Seven

I tried not to, but I couldn't help myself. I just had to get back to my earthly house to see what Saul was up to. I think part of me wanted to prove Denise wrong about my 'guardian angel' role. I admit I felt a little funny about tailing him like a celestial P.I., but this wasn't spying. It was supervision, for his own good.

I found Saul and Mary Lynn clutched in an embrace on the couch in the living room. Discarded clothing littered the floor: a blouse here, trousers there. The rust-colored sport jacket lay draped over the back of a dining room chair. Half-empty wine glasses imprinted the wood of the cocktail table with condensation rings that went unnoticed by the busy couple on the sofa.

Saul's voice came soft and ragged as Mary Lynn nuzzled his ear. "I think we better call it a night."

"It's early," Mary Lynn whispered, her hands roaming his back. She didn't miss a beat.

"No, really, M.L., I think it's time you got going."

Mary Lynn drew back and searched his face. Her always-perfect hair was tousled, but it only succeeded in making her look like a Playboy centerfold. I thought back to when Saul and I were young lovers. My hair never became sexily mussed; it stuck out like bristles on a Fuller brush. 'Nice hair, Brillo-head,' he'd tease.

Mary Lynn stroked his cheek. "Hey, it's okay. I know what you're going through. You feel disloyal to Judith, and I understand that. But can your memories of her give you what I can?" She took his hand and placed it over her breast. "Judith's gone, but I'm here. I won't let you be lonely," she breathed, running her tongue around the rim of his ear. She disengaged herself and pulled her tank top over her head, her eyes never leaving his.

My heart sank to the vicinity of my ankles.

Then a cold knot of fear twined in my stomach. Something about this scenario didn't seem right, and I don't mean Saul and Mary Lynn having an affair. A peculiar feeling—intuition, if you will—told me that Saul was on some kind of collision course with fate, and Mary Lynn was at the wheel.

My gut instincts were usually on the mark, but I wasn't convinced that this premonition wasn't at least partially based on jealousy. The one thing I was sure of was that Saul needed me, more than either of us realized. I knew I should take it slow, give myself a chance to shed these proprietary vestiges left over from my earthly emotions before I thought about helping Saul, but that would take too long. Saul needed me now. I didn't know exactly why yet, but that didn't matter. It just mattered that I be there for him. And if watching over Saul meant that I would be seeing a lot of him together with Mary Lynn, I had better start getting used to it, without recriminations.

Max and Ginger scratched at the back door from the outside, wanting in. I took that as my cue to exit. Even accountants are entitled to some privacy.

To take my mind off the unsettling image of Mary Lynn and Saul in a lip lock, I decided to go down to level Four and see Justin. Since that first meeting, I'd gone down there several times to visit, each time learning more about the lower levels and about Justin himself. There was something about him that drew me, a gentleness behind the tough-guy exterior. I sensed that if you peeled back the insolent, crass layers, you'd find a sad boy looking to be loved. There had to be some fundamental good in someone whose positive qualities shone through no matter how hard he tried to mask them. I had to be careful not to let on that I saw right through his façade, though. If he learned I had blown his cover, I suspected our friendship would end as quickly as it began.

I found him leaning against his front door jamb, smoking, as usual. He ignored the jaunty wave I threw him. I couldn't tell if it was deliberate or if he just hadn't noticed me yet. He tossed the cigarette onto the littered ground and methodically ground out the glowing butt. He jammed both hands in his jacket pockets and started down the street in the opposite direction.

My jaw fell. No way could he have missed me; he'd purposely ignored me. Perhaps I'd come at a bad time. I was willing–barely–to make allowances. His no-nonsense personality now bordered on plain rudeness. Anger bubbled up inside, tinged with a little embarrassment at his rebuff. I had anticipated a warm welcome, but here I had been avoided like the plague.

From halfway down the street, Justin stopped and called out to me. "Well? Are you coming or not?"

From Justin Caso, this was tantamount to a formal invitation. I hurried to catch up to him.

On level Four the perpetually overcast skies never cleared. The oily, wet streets never dried. Think Seattle in the Twilight Zone. The shabby buildings were propped against one another on hard-packed dirt through which rivulets of water carved miniature canals. Sparse, scraggly weeds made up most of the plant life here.

The depressing environment made me appreciate level Seven all the more. Once upon a lifetime, I might have been where Justin is now. Could that explain the kinship I felt with him? I couldn't think of any other reason for wanting to be with him. He wasn't particularly pleasant company. At times, he was downright nasty. Yet underneath it all, we understood each other, and I knew I could help bring out the good qualities he tried so hard to bury.

He picked up on my mood right away. "You're not Miss Perky Pollyanna today. What's up?"

"My husband is dating someone."

"So? He had to get some sometime."

"It's not that. It's whom he's dating."

"Oh, *whom*. Don't you like *whom*?"

I counted to ten. "I like her fine. We've known her for years, as a matter of fact."

Justin shrugged and fumbled in his pocket for a smoke. "Then what's the problem?"

Ah, the sixty-four thousand dollar question. "I wish I knew. I can't really put my finger on it. Saul just seems…different."

"Different. You mean happy. And you can't deal with that."

"That's not true," I protested. "Of course I want my husband to be happy."

"Don't bullshit me, Ms. J. You want him all mopey and hangdog, pining away for you. Why don't you admit it?"

"Absolutely not true."

His mouth twitched. "Relax. Life is short; you oughta know that better than most. Let him have his jollies while he can. It don't mean he wasn't into you."

He knew he was right, and he knew that I knew it. It was supremely aggravating to have this greaser from three Levels below me spouting wisdom. To his credit, he didn't say, "I told you so."

We walked around a little longer so that he could show me more of level Four, but there wasn't much to see. Except for the small settlements scattered around, there wasn't anything beyond the occasional scraggly tree and underbrush. The dusty emptiness made me long for home. I could take the bleak environment only in small doses.

Before I left, Justin cautioned me against watching over Saul. "You'll only see things that'll piss you off," he said. I knew he meant well, but I doubted that Justin Caso had much experience with guardian angels. He had no clue of what Saul and I had together, our deep commitment to each other. But I would show him.

And while I was at it, I might show Mary Lynn, too.

Chapter Eight

Suse J's house was right on the way to the level Seven Chocolate Festival, so I stopped by to pick her up. This was my first time at the annual event and I really looked forward to it. Dedicated chocoholic that I am, I didn't have to worry anymore about the usual reprisals of indulgence. Weight gain and complexion problems are non-issues up Here. Now that's what I call heaven.

When we entered the Social Hall, I gasped. Tables lined the entire perimeter, laden with endless varieties of the purest chocolate that never melted anywhere but in your mouth. We merged into the crowd of spirits milling around, sampling the various concoctions and chatting. New friends were made and old friends reunited ("You look so familiar. Did you go down on the *Titanic*?"). Off to one side, Gilda Radner, John Belushi, and Phil Hartman argued good-naturedly with John Candy and Chris Farley about which SNL cast was the best.

I took a bite of a chocolate truffle that tasted as smooth as a Nat King Cole ballad. Suse J laughed at the blissful expression on my face, and I stuck out my tongue at her.

"You two are having entirely too much fun over here." A tiny young woman stood beside us with arms akimbo.

Suse J shrieked in delight and the two hugged. "Chevron!"

"In the flesh...well, not really."

Suse J caught the curious look on my face. "Judith, this is Siobhan O'Malley." She turned to Siobhan. "Judith is a recent arrival to level Seven."

"Nice to meet you." Siobhan had no trace of the Irish brogue I expected.

"Likewise," I said with a smile.

"Siobhan spent several lifetimes as Irish men and women, so she kept her Irish name up Here," Suse J added.

"Yeah, never mind that my last life was in Ames, Iowa."

"Did I hear wrong, or did Suse just call you 'Chevron'?" I asked.

"You heard right."

"Old joke," Suse J put in.

"It's the name," Siobhan explained. "People unfamiliar with Gaelic names really butcher it. If they see it written down, they pronounce it 'See-ob-han.' If they hear it spoken, they think it's 'Chiffon'–which is really the closest to being correct–or 'Shebang.' 'Chevron' is one of the first variations I ever heard, so it became an inside joke."

Just then Suse J did a double-take. She stood on tiptoes and waved at someone at the other end of the hall.

"Excuse me for a minute," she said. "I've been trying for weeks to track Oliver down. You two go on getting acquainted and I'll be right back."

The two of us left to ourselves, diminutive Siobhan gave me a cheery smile. She couldn't have stood taller than four feet ten inches. Her clothes might have come from the pre-teen department, though I figured she was probably around twenty-two. I took an immediate liking to this girl who was so easy in her own skin that she put everyone around her at ease. Very unusual for someone who looked so young.

"If you don't mind my asking, Siobhan, how old are you?"

"Sixteen."

Even younger than I thought. She had a dignity that most earthly teenagers don't even recognize, much less carry.

"Does that surprise you?"

"Well, yes, it does. But you probably get that reaction a lot."

"Only from new arrivals."

"*Touché*. Would it be too obnoxious to ask how you came to die so young?"

"Not at all." She leaned over the long table next to us and selected a square of dark chocolate to pop in her mouth. Brushing non-existent crumbs from her hands, she cautioned, "Brace yourself. It's probably the most ridiculous story you'll ever hear."

That's what you think. "It can't be that bad."

"Oh, I'd say so. My high school class took a bus trip to Chicago over spring break. We were on the interstate when an eighteen-wheeler coming the other way lost control and plowed into us."

I squeezed my eyes shut to blot out the graphic mental picture of the ensuing crash. "That'll do it. But a bus accident is nothing to be embarrassed about."

She arched her brow. "How many crash victims have you met who were on the john at the moment of impact?"

I tightened my lips together to suppress the mirth threatening to erupt. "I'll admit that's pretty undignified."

"It's the ultimate indignity! When I departed the body and saw the rescue workers staring at it outside what was left of the lavatory, I nearly died all over again. My jeans were still down around my knees."

I couldn't hold it in anymore; I had to laugh.

"See what I mean?"

"I'm sorry," I choked. "The real reason I'm laughing is…well, wait until I tell you how *I* died…"

Siobhan and I got together frequently after that. We acknowledged an affinity with each other, souls who knew firsthand what it's like taking the road less traveled. We both had fallen into more than a few potholes along the way, but I never let her know how much I preferred dying from static laxatives to expiration by urination.

A few weeks later, I hurried home after a shift in the Jungle–the moniker Suse J had bestowed on the Animal Domain–anxious to change into something not decorated with dog hair before I went to check on Saul. It had been a while since I paid my last visit to him, the one where I saw for myself that his relationship with Mary Lynn had blossomed into something far beyond W-2s and escrow holdings.

I was so preoccupied with thoughts of Saul that I didn't see Siobhan walking towards me.

She grabbed my arms to avert collision. "Whoa! Where's the fire?"

"Sorry, guess I am a little distracted."

"A little? You're in another world...so to speak."

"That's original, Siobhan."

"You were expecting maybe Joan Rivers? Now, where are you going so hell-bent for leather?"

"I'm going down to see my husband, but I need to change clothes first." I brushed fur from my sleeve.

She frowned. "Again, Jude? I though we agreed that this obsession with your husband isn't healthy."

"What do you mean 'again'? I'd hardly call it an obsession; I haven't seen him in almost a month."

"Isn't that only because every time you dropped in on him, he was with the blonde bombshell?"

"Yeah, well, I'm no *voyeuse*."

"Jude, I don't mean to interfere, but..."

I knew what was coming. Siobhan meant well, but she was definitely interfering. She needed a diversion.

"Hey, why don't you come with me?"

"Now?"

"Of course now. If you have a look at Saul for

yourself, maybe you'll understand why I need to take care of him."

She peered at me as if trying to find a hidden agenda. She must have decided I had none because she consented. "But if things start getting intimate, don't expect me to stick around."

"Don't worry. I won't be sticking around, either."

I linked my arm through hers and hurried us both to my house where I shed my work clothes and slipped into a striped silk caftan that had been a welcome-home gift from Ashraf.

Very soon, Siobhan and I were in the living room of the home I had shared with Saul. He was nowhere to be seen and the house was deathly quiet. Siobhan settled herself on the sofa and leafed through the copy of *Newsweek* lying on the cocktail table while I checked out the bedroom. The door was ajar, and I held my breath as I eased it all the way open. Ginger and Max were the only occupants, napping peacefully on the bed.

Siobhan had been only too right about my last attempted visits to Saul. Every time I looked in on him, he was busily practicing indoor sports with Mary Lynn. Talk about your lousy timing.

So I cooled the visits for a bit, hoping that a break from routine would improve my chances of finding him alone, or even with somebody else. He was spending altogether too much time with one person. You'd think he'd want to broaden his horizons a bit before getting serious so fast. I mean, monogamy is fine, but he deserved more than a rebound relationship. That's all Mary Lynn was–a rebound person, a transitional girlfriend, a fuck buddy.

Siobhan looked up as I drifted back into the living room. I shook my head in answer to her unspoken question.

"Now what?" she asked.

"Now we go and find him."

"But he could be anywhere."

"If I concentrate hard, we'll travel to wherever he is. Here, take my hand."

I was a whiz at spiritual transportation now, like I'd been riding the energy waves all my life. I didn't doubt we'd home in on Saul with very little trouble. We closed our eyes and Saul's face bloomed in my mind, minus the moustache. I focused on his hazel eyes, more green than brown; his lean frame; the lock of straight black hair that continuously fell over his forehead.

I pressed Siobhan's hand as a signal to open our eyes. I was surprised to see us still in Saul's living room.

She stated the obvious. "Nothing happened."

This hadn't occurred before. "Let me give it one more try." I took up Siobhan's hand again, squeezed my eyes shut and pictured Saul, this time with that silly moustache.

Within seconds I knew we had made it. I pressed Siobhan's hand and opened my own eyes.

"It worked," she exulted. "What did you do differently that time?"

"It's a little complicated to explain," I hedged. Turning

in a slow circle, I asked, "Where are we?" A rather foolish and transparent diversion tactic, since it was clear where we were.

We stood on a high ridge overlooking a valley. People bustled about a nearby area littered with metal poles and expanses of canvas sheeting. They all had the rugged physiques and tanned faces of outdoors enthusiasts.

Siobhan nudged me and nodded toward the edge of the cliff. "Look."

A trim woman appeared to be attached to what looked like some kind of flying equipment. Clad in a skin-tight jumpsuit, her body looked honed of finely planed wood. She began running toward the precipice, looking for all the world like a modern-day Icarus. As she approached the cliff's edge, the wind lifted the wings of the apparatus, pulling her into the emptiness beyond. She caught a thermal and rose without effort into the sky.

As soon as she soared off, I realized I'd been holding my breath during the entire scene. High places were definitely outside my comfort zone. I tried to exhale quietly so Siobhan wouldn't notice.

She walked up to the very edge of the cliff for a closer look, then turned to me and beckoned. "Come on."

"No, thanks. I can see fine from back here."

"Judith, you dope, you won't fall off. You don't have a body that can fall, remember?"

"Old phobias never die; they just evolve to a higher plane."

"Don't think you can joke your way out of this one. It's time to evolve this phobia right out of your plane," she said firmly.

She had a point. My old fears still had a claim on me and if I wanted to be rid of them, I had to stop feeding them.

"Okay, here I come." I straightened my shoulders, lifted my head, and marched to where Siobhan stood about six inches from the edge of the abyss. The closer I got, the more my confidence flagged and the slower my steps became.

Siobhan shook her head. "You're hopeless." With a sixteen-year-old's typical impatience, she reached out and yanked my arm, causing me to lose footing on the loose dirt. I went sailing into the void, instinctively treading air with my arms and legs as though I were in water. I hung there, suspended. Siobhan floated over next to me, laughing.

I glowered at her. "What did you do that for?"

"Because I knew you wouldn't get over this height thing until I proved you wouldn't fall."

I folded my arms across my chest. "Okay, you made your point. Now how do I get back there?" I pointed to the cliff.

"Swim."

"Swim?"

"Swim," Siobhan repeated.

I started to breaststroke, feeling clumsy and a little foolish. Sure enough, I made my way back to the rocky cliff, close enough to step onto solid ground.

Siobhan gloated her triumph. "See? That wasn't so bad."

"I suppose not. But why couldn't I just use teleportation?"

"You could, but then you wouldn't get to watch anything. It's too instantaneous. If you want to check out the scenery, you have to take the scenic route."

She pointed toward the hang gliders floating over the valley. "Doesn't that look like fun?"

I opened my mouth to tell her what I really thought it looked like, but abruptly closed it again. It *was* kind of fun just to hang there in midair like that. How much more fun would it be to soar like an eagle?

"No, darling, the strap goes this way."

Siobhan and I both turned toward the all-too-familiar voice that came from behind us. There stood Saul, trussed up like a Thanksgiving turkey, with Mary Lynn adjusting the restraining gear on his hang glider.

Siobhan's jaw fell. "Omigod."

"You can say that again. What does Saul think he's doing?"

"*That's* Saul?"

"Yes, that's Saul. And there's the ubiquitous blonde bombshell. Why do you sound so funny?"

"Judith, you should have told me Saul was involved with *her*. I wouldn't have given you so much grief for checking up on him the way you do."

"I did tell you."

"You always called her 'M.L.' or 'blonde bombshell.'"

Come to think of it, I don't believe I ever mentioned Mary Lynn by name to Siobhan.

"I didn't know you were referring to Mary Lynn Walker," she said in dismay.

"You know her?"

"I never made the connection…Jude, that woman is bad news."

"Tell me about it. But how do you know her?"

"We were sisters in my last life."

She had to be teasing. "Oh, you want to play *Six Degrees of Kevin Bacon*, huh? Okay, now connect yourself to Eminem."

Siobhan drew in a sharp breath. "I'm serious."

One look at the fear in her eyes and I knew she *was* serious. "But, Siobhan, Mary Lynn isn't from Iowa. She grew up in West Virginia."

"I'm not surprised she would lie about that. After what she did, I'm sure she didn't want her past catching up with her. I'll bet she never told you she had a sister, did she?"

I thought back. "Well, no, but I don't recall ever asking about her family, either."

"When I was thirteen, our house caught on fire. A fire that Mary Lynn started."

"What are you saying, she's a pyromaniac? An arsonist?"

"Not exactly. The fire started by accident from her cigarette. Our parents didn't allow her to smoke, so she sneaked cigarettes whenever they weren't home. One evening while they were out, she fell asleep with a lit cigarette in her hand."

"But you both survived."

Siobhan nodded. "She was lying on the living room sofa, underneath a big picture window. The firemen found her right away and got her out, but I was asleep upstairs."

"I don't understand. Firemen have oxygen masks; they could have gotten to you just as quickly."

She hesitated. "When the firemen asked Mary Lynn if anyone else was in the house, she said no."

I gasped. How could Mary Lynn do such a thing, and to her own sister? "That was heinous of her, I grant you, but wouldn't the firemen have gone in anyway, just to double check?"

"They did, but not until after Mary Lynn's *Camille* performance. They fawned all over her, giving her oxygen and everything...they didn't go back inside the house for a good ten minutes. By then I'd managed to get out on my own."

"How?"

"All I remember is waking up, choking. It was like breathing acid, and the smoke was so thick, I couldn't see. I crawled out of bed and searched with my hands for the window, choking and coughing. I felt like my head was being squeezed in a vise, and I knew I was going to pass out. Thank God the window sash had been up already, or I wouldn't have had the strength or time to fumble with it. I sat on the floor and kicked the screen out. Somehow I managed to drag myself over the ledge and I just let myself fall out of the window. Broke my pelvis and an arm, but I survived."

My mouth hung slack in horrified disbelief. "How did Mary Lynn explain herself afterwards?"

"She said she forgot I was there. Thought I was spending the night at a friend's house." Siobhan gave a lopsided grin and rolled her eyes. "Yeah, right. Nobody else bought it, either. My parents put her in a residential treatment center for a couple of years. She came home 'cured,' but I had my doubts."

"You speak of this so calmly, Siobhan, like it happened to someone else."

She turned her face away to gaze out over the valley. "In a way, it did. I forgave my sister long ago, but I still know her for what she is." She turned back to me, eyes etched with concern. "Watch out for her, Judith. There's something...not quite right about Mary Lynn."

"Okay, here we go! GERONIMO!" Mary Lynn's voice broke in as she and Saul took off in tandem on a glider, Mary Lynn on top. Typical.

"Yee-ha," Saul exulted as the currents took them skyward. "This is fantastic!"

All thoughts of Siobhan's amazing revelation fled in the face of what I saw. Saul McBride, the man who wouldn't ride a roller coaster because he didn't trust the integrity of its maintenance, was hang gliding. Cautious to a fault, Saul used to lecture me on the dangers of allowing the washing machine to run while we weren't home. Back the car out of the garage without the seat belt fastened? Unthinkable. Yet here he was, moustache and all, riding the wind like Evel Knievel. I tried to absorb the reality of it.

I watched spellbound as they circled the valley a few times, descending on each orbit. Saul attempted a steep turn that brought them perilously close to the jagged cliff and I clutched Siobhan's arm. I didn't need my own eyes to see how close they actually came to sideswiping the rock face; Mary Lynn's high-pitched shriek said it all. Her counter-maneuver should have been subtle enough to guide them gently back on course. Reflexes rattled by the near miss, she over-compensated, sending them straight for the opposite cliff.

When the craft slid away from the rocks and continued on its gradual descent, I heaved a sigh of relief. The glider spiraled on, and I grabbed Siobhan's hand. "Come on, we're going down to watch the landing."

Leaving her no time to protest, I focused every ounce of concentration on the image of Saul making contact with *terra firma*. In the next second, we stood among the group at the landing area. The throng watched Saul and Mary Lynn approach the target marked with a giant X, giving it a wide berth. Someone–a veteran glider or perhaps another instructor–urged the crowd back even more to give the first-timer extra room.

Mary Lynn gripped a cord in each hand, giving one or

the other a tug to make slight corrections in their glide path. They seemed to be coming in very fast. In a split second they were so low I was positive they'd never walk away from the landing. At the last moment, Mary Lynn pushed out hard on the sides of the uprights that formed the A-frame of the glider. The nose angled up sharply, bringing the craft to a stop and lifting Saul and Mary Lynn to an upright position. They safely touched down.

A cheer from the crowd went up as Mary Lynn extracted herself and unbuckled Saul's harness. He climbed out of the apparatus very proud of himself. I noted a decided swagger to his walk, most un-McBride-like. He received any number of congratulatory back slaps and hair rumplings for a successful first flight.

He caught Mary Lynn in an elated embrace and whirled her around. "Baby, that was great! When do you think I'll be ready to solo?"

"Down, tiger, down." Mary Lynn laughed. "That was just an orientation flight. You'll have to go through the formal training before you can solo."

"Where do I sign up?"

Siobhan eyed me with sympathy. She knew me well enough by now to see that this troubled me. I didn't recognize this Saul McBride.

With the impeccable timing of friendship, she extended her hand in a tacit invitation to return to our own world. I took it and we closed our eyes. A nanosecond later, we were back on level Seven, near one of the great fountains.

The gurgling sound of the water soothed me, and soon I felt some peace return.

After a minute or two, Siobhan broke the silence. "At least they were doing something outside of bed."

"For a change. So now it seems my choices are either to watch my husband while he's with another woman or trying to get himself killed."

"Nobody says you have to watch at all."

"Come on, Siobhan, you said yourself that Mary Lynn is trouble. I have to protect Saul now more than ever, from himself as well as from her. It's obvious he isn't thinking very clearly about what he's doing."

"Jude," she pleaded, "you know you can't save Saul from himself or anyone else. He's got to do what he's got to do."

Now even Siobhan was lecturing me? Resentment flashed on my face like a neon sign and Siobhan backed off. She suggested returning to her house for a chocolate break. "I made brownies this morning."

I deliberated for a moment. "With nuts?"

"Is there any other way?"

Chapter Nine

Over the next few months, I watched my husband transform from couch potato to sports-loving adventurer. Under Mary Lynn's persuasive tutelage, Saul took up skiing and SCUBA diving. The money from the sale of his father's business, heretofore hoarded in anticipation of a Rainy Day, was now freely spent on rafting trips down the Colorado River and snowboarding lessons at Chamonix. Mary Lynn reassured him on a regular basis that she was keeping a watchful eye on his investments and would alert him if they needed to tone down the spending. Since their excursions maintained a steady bi-monthly pace, I could only assume the market must have been very bullish.

For someone who used to have trouble dragging Saul outside for a simple bike ride, this was a bitter pill to swallow. Once, I had tried to talk him into a cruise through Antarctica, but he wouldn't even consider it. Now he continent-hopped as if born to the purple. Who watched over Max and Ginger while he was out jet setting, I'd like to know?

I shared my concerns with Ashraf one day over tea. He often came down from his residence on level Eight to see me and his other charges on Seven. Our relationship was now more equitable. When we visited, it was as friends rather than mentor and protégée. He would always be my spirit guide, of course, but the warp and woof of our dynamic continually adapted.

"I don't know," I sighed. "Saul is so completely changed from the man I married. He's reveling in this new life of activity, while I could hardly ever pry him away from the television. Had marriage to me been so confining? I *tried* to interest him in new things, but he just..."

"People handle grief in very different ways, Judith."

"Hiking in the Swiss Alps is grieving? I don't think so."

"You have said yourself that you did not want Saul to cease living just because you did." He eyed me with suspicion. "Is it possible your distress is borne of a jealousy you cannot release?"

"No, Ash, I'm beyond that now."

"Are you sure? This accountant you speak of seems to have a powerful physical effect on your husband. She is beautiful, you say?"

"She's gorgeous. Look, no matter the reason, she's got Saul taking all kinds of risks and I don't like it."

"Ah, at last we come to the heart of the matter."

My lip curled in anticipation of another lecture. I reached for my teacup and stirred another sugar cube into the already sugared orange pekoe. I took a sullen sip and braced myself.

"You cannot do anything about it, you know. You

cannot protect Saul from himself or anyone else," Ash reminded me.

I'd heard that before. "Then what good am I if I can't help the people I love?"

"Perhaps that is not your divine purpose. Your only responsibility for the time being is to love yourself enough to expand your own soul to its greatest potential."

I took another sip and set the teacup down again. Tepid.

"My dear Judith, I do not relish preaching to you, especially when it is the same sermon time after time."

You can say *that* again. "It's not exactly a day at the beach for me, either."

"Then will you promise me something?"

"What?"

"I want you to promise that you will allow Saul to resolve his own fate, and that you will concentrate more on yourself. Will you do that? For me?"

Something in his voice told me this was very important to him. Ashraf had never asked me for anything before...and I shouldn't forget that his elevation to spirit guide and level Eight indicated a certain wisdom.

"All right, Ash. I promise."

He grinned his pleasure, white teeth gleaming.

I added a cautionary note. "But that doesn't mean I won't keep tabs on Saul. I'll look, but I won't touch."

Ash poured some fresh tea and raised his cup in a toast. "You drive a hard bargain, Judith."

Our cups clinked.

* * *

I was as good as my word. It wasn't easy, but I managed to wean myself down to monthly visits to Saul, resisting the urge to sneak an extra peek. Remembering Ashraf's admonition to let Saul learn his own life lessons, I clamped my mouth shut when he broke a leg barefooting in Mazatlán. I watched him hobble around the house on crutches and reiterated my promise, even when Mary Lynn pressured him to find new homes for Max and Ginger. "A man in your condition, living alone, is in no position to care for even one pet, let alone two," she reasoned.

I expected Saul to refuse to capitulate on this matter, but capitulate he did, which infuriated me. Instead of the self-confident, independent man I'd always admired, I suddenly had to deal with a milksop who couldn't see when he was being manipulated. He cared about Max and Ginger as much as I did. How could he set them aside so easily?

I had to give Mary Lynn credit: she was one smooth operator. She had Saul convinced that giving away Max and Ginger was in the dogs' best interest. After all, she explained, the poor things spent half the time boarding in a kennel when she and Saul traveled, right? Wouldn't it be better to find them a new home where they would have more long-term stability?

I lost a modicum of respect for my husband after that. One of the things I had fallen in love with was how sure Saul always was of everything. He knew who he was and what he wanted. Granted, this confidence translated into a stubborn streak that at times drove me nuts, but I much preferred a headstrong Saul to the person I saw now. He'd become an extension of Mary Lynn's idea of what a man should be: pliable to her wants and fulfilling only of her needs. I failed to see why Mary Lynn would even want to be with such a doormat.

The answer, of course, was in Saul's bank account.

Micaela, bless her, came to the rescue. Devoted friend that she was, she had made a point of keeping in touch with Saul after my death. At first he welcomed the companionship. Her phone calls and the occasional drink after work eased his loneliness. Their mutual grief was a comfortable place. Both had loved and lost the same person. Often they talked long into the night, reminiscing about good times the four of us had and laughing over things I had said or done.

Gerry Pressman understood their need to grieve together, and never complained about the many hours his wife spent with Saul. Sometimes I wondered if their common sorrow might turn into something more, a prospect I viewed as problematic but utterly predictable. Had Micaela been single, it would have been my greatest wish that they fall in love. They would have been good for each other.

Enter the blonde bombshell. Once Mary Lynn got her hooks into Saul, Micaela saw him less and less. Any contact between them came at Micaela's initiation. Mary

Lynn so completely mesmerized Saul that he no longer made time for his wife's best friend, who had been a good and loyal friend to him, as well. If this hurt Mic's feelings, she never let on. She continued to phone Saul–even though she usually got his voice mail–to find out how he was doing and ask if he needed anything. Even after he began refusing her invitations to dinner, she stayed in touch with him. It was so like her.

I was never more grateful to Micaela than when she offered to adopt Max and Ginger. During one of their increasingly rare after-work get-togethers, Saul mentioned his plans to get rid of them. If he didn't find a taker pretty soon, he would have to leave them at the local shelter. He and M.L. were flying to Europe the following week and he wanted the matter settled before they left.

Knowing how upset I would have been at the idea of my dogs being cast off like old shoes, Micaela told Saul that she would take them in. He was immensely relieved. He hadn't really *wanted* to turn them over to the shelter, but M.L. had become so insistent.

One evening, not long after their return from Europe, I dropped in on Saul for my monthly visit. Right away I knew something was up. I expected to find him and Mary Lynn holed up in the bedroom, necking on the couch, or out for the evening. For once, the candles were not lit and clothes weren't strewn around the room. In fact, the living room was empty, so I followed a beacon of light into the dining room. The dimmer switch controlling the chandelier's brightness was turned all the way up, the better to pore over the travel brochures spread out on the oval dining table.

I listened in amazement as Mary Lynn gave Saul the hard sell on this latest adventure. She leaned toward him in her seat and spoke animatedly. "Think of it, darling. How many people can say they've done this?"

"It does look incredible," Saul conceded, picking up a pamphlet to study. "But why New Zealand? It's such a long way. Aren't there places closer to home where we can bungee jump?"

"But this is the Everest of bungee sites. People plan for years to go to Skipper's Canyon Bridge. What would you rather do, jump off a cherry picker at the county fair?"

"Depends which county."

"Very funny."

"Seriously, M.L., I don't know that we should do this at all."

"You didn't want to go sky diving at first, either," she reminded him. "And now you love it."

"I do love it, and I don't think anything can top the rush of jumping out of a perfectly good airplane. So let's just leave it at that, shall we?"

Mary Lynn slumped back in her chair. "Where's that coming from? You're beginning to sound like a bore again."

"'Again'?"

"I didn't mean it that way," she back-pedaled. "I just thought the new Saul would love a trip like this–the Saul who's open to trying new things and living life to the fullest."

"You really mean the Saul you rescued from being a hopeless loser, don't you?"

Mary Lynn slid out of her chair and went to him, sitting sideways on his lap. She put her arms around his neck and murmured into his ear. "I mean the Saul who drives me so crazy I can't keep my hands off him." She teased the fringe of his moustache with her tongue and softly kissed his lips. "Won't you give New Zealand a try?"

"We just got back from Monte Carlo."

Mary Lynn swung a leg over his so that she now sat facing him. "Please? For me?" Her fingers twirled a lock of his hair.

"We're spending an awful lot of money, M.L." His voice was thick.

She began to move sinuously on his lap. "Let me worry about that," she whispered. "Don't I always take care of you?"

Saul groaned and stood up with Mary Lynn in his arms. "I know how you can take care of me right now..."

As they crossed to the bedroom, an unnerving heaviness began to well up inside me. Trepidation blossomed in my gut and spread like a stain to my extremities. Negative energy was the culprit, and it could only be coming from Saul and Mary Lynn. And it wasn't the sex that bothered me; something about this proposed exploit spelled disaster for my husband. I could feel it.

This one would put him in real danger. A bungee jumping trip to New Zealand wouldn't be just a lark; it would be suicide. I didn't know how or why, I just knew that if Saul went on this trip, it would be the end of him. I wish I could say that I had the power to see into the future, but the explanation isn't that easy. As grateful as I was that he wasn't gung-ho on the idea, I also knew how persuasive Mary Lynn could be. But he *must not* cave on this one.

Suddenly I wanted very much to go home, and not just because Saul and Mary Lynn were at it again. I felt so... peculiar. Something was very wrong.

Anxious now to get out of there, I closed my eyes and concentrated on level Seven. But something here was wrong, too. I had a sensation of running and running but getting nowhere, as if my shoes were stuck in molasses. The sound of rushing air whooshed past my ears. My astral trips were normally instantaneous, but not this time. I squeezed my eyes tighter, trying to stay focused on the restorative atmosphere of Seven.

I opened my eyes, expecting the familiar appointments of my own living room, or at least my own neighborhood. Instead, I found myself in a desolate outdoor basketball court, the inner-city kind enclosed by a rusting chain-link fence. The basketball hoops had no nets, and dry leaves rasped across the court's cracked surface. Beyond the fence, a graffiti-spattered concrete retaining wall shouted *kitchen's hell, welcome to your nightmare,* and *no, this isn't Newark.*

"Hey."

Justin stood on the other side of the fence, his fingers hooked through the chain links like a prisoner in his cell. "You dint tell me you was coming, Ms. J. Whatchoo doing here?"

I wondered the same thing.

"There ain't no basketballs, even if the hoops had nets," he continued, as if my main concern was that we wouldn't be able to get a game of pick-up.

Why *was* I here?

Justin walked the perimeter of the fence to meet me by the gate. He helped himself to a cigarette and regarded me for a second before extending the pack. In a fit of nervous rebellion, I reached out to take one. He jerked the pack out of my reach and laughed. *Gotcha!* I shot him a we-are-not-amused look.

"Okay, okay." He held out the pack again and allowed me to pull out a cigarette. He didn't offer me a light. I caught his hand and used the glowing end of his cigarette to light my own. Our hands shook, but it came from my own trembling.

I took a deep drag and exhaled with the practiced air of a dedicated smoker, even though I hadn't had a cigarette since I had been an earthbound teenager. Back then I hadn't taken to it, but this first celestial cigarette gave me a taste of what nicotine addicts have been raving about all these years. I pulled the woody-tasting smoke deep into my lungs, rewarded with a cool rush that calmed the trembling and cleared my head. The paradox of a heaven that included something associated with disease, death, and children of a lesser God struck me.

"So all of a sudden you're a smoker," Justin scoffed. "You wanna tell me where you been to make you act so squirrelly?"

I blew out smoke with pretended indifference. "Oh, I just thought I'd pop down and see what you're up to."

"And just happened to end up in a deserted basketball court. C'mon, Ms. J., I can tell a short landing when I see one. If you was really coming to see me, you'd go to my front yard like you always do."

I said nothing. I took another drag and relaxed against the fence, leaning my head back against the chilly metal.

"You wanna tell me about it?"

Feeling like the homegirl I wasn't, I copped a squat and flicked ashes off the end of the cigarette, so hungry for moral support from any quarter that I assimilated into Justin's world. He sat down on the damp concrete and leaned back against the fence, stretching out his denim-clad legs in front. He cocked an eyebrow at me, waiting.

I told him of Mary Lynn's plan to take Saul bungee jumping in New Zealand, glossing over the specifics of her sales technique.

"Whatchoo so upset about? From what you say, he ain't even agreed to go yet."

And you haven't seen Mary Lynn's powers of persuasion... "I'm afraid he will. And if he goes ahead with this ridiculous idea, it will be his last."

"Yeah? What makes you so sure?"

"I don't know how I know, Justin. I just feel it in my essence."

"Say what?"

"My gut. I have a gut feeling about it."

"Hang on a minute. Even if Saul does go to this bungee place and buys the farm that way, it's his karma. You can't do nothing about it."

"That's just the point, Justin, I can. I don't have to sit and twiddle my thumbs while my husband goes on a suicide mission."

Justin morphed into a Cary Grant caricature. "Ju-dy, Ju-dy, Ju-dy," he clucked, shaking his head in disappointment. "Don't go off and do something you'll be sorry for later. Don't be thinking you can change your old man's destiny."

"I don't want to change it; I want to prolong it. I don't want him to break his neck over some jackass idea of Mary Lynn's. Is that so terrible?"

"Yeah, more than you realize. You wanna end up like me, living in a shit hole like this? 'Cause if you try to mix in Saul's life, it'll knock you down a rung or two up Here. Lemme tell you, Ms. J., you won't like the kind you'd be chilling with on this level…or worse."

"Oh, you're not so bad," I teased. "We're friends, aren't we?"

"Friends. Maybe you don't wanna be friends with me. You don't really know me."

"I doubt you could tell me anything that would shock me, Justin."

"Oh, yeah? I did some things in my last go-around on earth that would tilt your tiara, lady."

"Such as?"

"Such as when I worked in the kitchen of this fancy-ass restaurant. They was really looking for a busboy but told me I dint have the 'right presentation' to be out front. Christ, was I pissed. They stuck me in the kitchen with some wetback who dint speak no English. He washed, I dried. And every once in a while I spit into the dishtowel. Gave the plates a real nice shine." Satisfaction tugged at the corners of Justin's mouth when he saw a horrified expression creep over my face.

I was determined not to let on just how much his words repulsed me. Instead, I tried to act unimpressed. "That's your idea of retaliation?" I scoffed. "The restaurant owner didn't even know about it, did he?"

"He dint have to. *I* knew it. It made me feel real fine."

He was enjoying himself now. "It gets better. Two years later I got booked for vagrancy. They gave me a choice: the slammer or the army. So I went in the army. Dint last too long there. Dint much like some asshole barking orders at me night and day. One afternoon I sneaked into the D.I.'s quarters and took a piss on his toothbrush. Man, you shoulda heard him the next morning. He made the whole unit PT extra hard and took away our weekend liberty, but it was worth it."

If discarnate spirits could possibly become nauseated, I would have lost it right then and there. Still I refused to give Justin the perverse satisfaction he looked for in shocking me. I swallowed hard. "What did they do, discharge you?"

"Yeah, but not because of that. They never did find out it was me." He chuckled at the memory. "That was about the same time the narcolepsy stuff started. I got out on a medical."

I cocked my head as though seeing him for the first time. "You know what, Justin? You're sick."

"I know. That's why I'm telling you all this. You don't want to do nothing stupid that could land you down here with souls like me. I'm telling you this 'cause I like you, Ms. J. I don't wanna see you screw up your soul growth. You interfere with your old man's destiny and that's just what you'll be doing. Take it from me; the Spirit Council will knock you down so fast it'll make your halo spin. I ain't hardly bullshitting you. You won't like it."

I looked at him, disgust replaced by astonishment at his diatribe. He looked back and for once, I could see no mockery in his eyes. In fact, his face had never looked more serious. In his own way, Justin really tried to do something he believed was for my own good. But it wasn't enough to make me change my mind about saving Saul.

"I appreciate your concern, Justin, but sometimes you've got to take chances. As Admiral Grace Hopper once said, 'A ship in port is safe, but that's not what ships are built for.'"

"Who the fuck is Grace Hopper and what kinda crap are you talking?"

"Grace Hopper was the first female U.S. Naval officer to–never mind. Listen, I know you mean well, but you just don't understand. If I don't stop Saul from doing this bungee jumping thing, something tells me he will die before he is supposed to. I just can't let that happen."

A shrill bark, a sound totally out of place for level Four, made my ears ring. Justin and I both turned in the direction of the sound and saw the dog running toward us.

"Melly?" I cried. "What are you doing here?"

"Jesus Christ," Justin muttered, backing up a couple of steps from the onrushing mutt.

"Don't worry; she won't hurt you. That's my dog, Melange. Though how she got here is–"

Melly didn't slow down, but about six feet away from us she braked her feet so sharply I thought her paw pads would scrape and burn. She looked like Fred Flintstone trying to stop his foot-powered car, and I would have laughed if it hadn't been for the bristling fur on her back and the low growl that came from her throat as she eyed Justin.

"Melly, that's no way to behave." I knelt down to pet her. "This is a friend. You don't have to be afraid of Justin."

Eyes never leaving him, Melly's lips curled back to expose the sharp teeth.

Justin stood his ground, less afraid now but still wary.

"Tell that goddamn mutt to lay off," he demanded.

"She wouldn't hurt a fly. I just don't understand. Here, Melly, say hello. Justin, hold out your hand for her to sniff."

He stuck out a tentative hand and I tried to nudge Melly toward him. The growling became a loud warning bark. Justin jerked back his hand. "I guess she don't like the look of my aura," he ventured, keeping a watchful eye on the dog's posture.

"Don't be silly. Even I haven't seen your aura."

"That don't mean it ain't there."

"How could Melly see an aura if I can't?"

Exasperation crossed his face. "Don't they teach you nothing up there in that fancy place you live? Animals can always see our auras. They got more pure instinct about souls than we'll ever have."

I looked down at Melly, who stared at Justin as closely as he did her. She had stopped growling but her back was still up. I tried again. "Melly, Justin is our friend."

Melly's lips curled back farther. The menacing growl returned. I blinked in utter disbelief. "I just don't get it."

"Maybe you better stop trying to get it and just get that mutt outta here," Justin said. "She's liable to pounce any minute."

"Melly would never–" But Melly *was* acting in a way I've never seen before and I couldn't promise she would never attack. At this point I didn't know what she was capable of. "Guess you're right. I'd better take her home now."

"Good idea." Justin reached deep into the pocket of his jeans and drew out a length of frayed rope, reminding me of a little Beaver Cleaver with a collection of odds and ends in his pockets. "Here, tie this around her collar. And step on it, I don't like the way she's still looking at me."

I attached the makeshift leash and pulled gently on it, but Melly's fixation on Justin did not easily break.

"Come on, girl," I urged.

"For chrissake, just yank on the rope and get her outta here," Justin shouted.

Though I wasn't about to do anything of the kind, Melly's behavior did point to the need for an immediate departure. I gave another gentle tug on the rope and implored, "Come *on*, Melly." She growled one last time and finally turned away from Justin to sniff the ground behind me.

Relieved, I tried to smooth things over. "I can't imagine why she's here and acting so weird. Listen, about that other stuff: everything will work out, you watch." Justin looked like he had more to say on the subject, but Melly's presence spared me from being further lectured. For once I actually got to have the last word with Justin Caso.

I waggled on the rope to get the dog's's attention. "Let's go, girl."

I closed my eyes to think both of us home, determined this time to get it right. "Be seeing you, Justin."

His voice came floating after me. "That's what I'm afraid of."

Chapter Ten

I made light of Justin's warning at the time, but his words left me wondering. Was it truly wrong to interfere in Saul's life, even if I might save it? Everyone seemed to think so. Siobhan thought I should stay out of it. Suse J, too.

After listening to Mary Lynn's enthusiastic description of their proposed destination in New Zealand, the answer was an unequivocal *no.*

Skipper's Canyon Bridge in Queenstown on New Zealand's south island is considered the bomb of bungee jumping sites, and with good reason. The lofty bridge spans a narrow, rocky canyon over the equally narrow Shotover River. The jump itself, however, is not the pinnacle of the excursion. There is a hair-raising jeep ride to the bridge, up a narrow mountain road unprotected by guardrails of any kind. Maybe this is supposed to get the adrenaline flowing and psych you up for the bungee jump off the bridge. The whole Skipper's Canyon experience culminates in a high-speed boat ride through the ravines of the serpentine river. The only thing keeping you from crashing into one of the many rock outcroppings is the skill of the boat captain.

Listening to Mary Lynn relate all this to Saul in her

pitch sessions, I decided she had lost all sense of reason. This trip wasn't adventurous; it was absurdly risky. Why she would want to put both of them in such danger was beyond me. More to the point, why would Saul even consider such an idea?

At this juncture, a logical question would be why I was so upset at the possibility of Saul's earthly life coming to an end. His death, albeit premature, meant he would be up Here with me that much sooner. So why wasn't I happy at the thought of an early reunion with my husband?

Believe me; I pondered that question long and hard. I even made a list of the advantages to Saul's spirit coming back to me before his time. He'd be rid of Mary Lynn, and she wouldn't be able to endanger or hurt him further. He wouldn't have to miss me anymore. We could work on our spiritual evolution together, maybe even reincarnate together.

In the end, I couldn't deny the simple fact that Saul deserved to live out this life to its fullest duration. No matter how much I would have loved to have him with me up Here, I just couldn't let it end because Mary Lynn had a death wish. Saul had too much to offer the world to have his life cut down short, even if he didn't realize it himself. At least *someone* did, and I was in a position to do something about it. Now I just had to come up with the best way to prevent him from traipsing off to New Zealand.

A few days and many chocolate bars later, I found a simple solution. Let Saul make the decision himself not to take the trip. He hadn't yet agreed to go. All he needed was a little subtle encouragement to call off the whole idea. The best way to do that, the only way, was to appeal to his subconscious.

I vacillated between mystical symbolism versus a clear-cut message of impending doom. In the end I opted for impending doom. If Saul couldn't even see through Mary Lynn's real-life machinations, a symbolic message would be equally lost on him.

I chose a night when Saul slept alone. Such occasions were rare, but at least Mary Lynn hadn't sold her condo. She may have taken over my husband's body and was working on his soul, but she hadn't yet moved into my house.

On this particular night, late enough for Saul to be sound asleep, I crept to his bedside. I don't know why I bothered to skulk; he wouldn't have heard me if I clanked a pair of cymbals next to his head. For some reason tiptoeing seemed appropriate.

As I entered our bedroom, I looked at the brocade slipper chair in the corner between the windows and the bed. We both used to toss the odd sweater or pair of jeans on it when too tired or too lazy to hang them up. It was the one thing that hadn't changed during Mary Lynn's redecorating frenzy. She had wasted no time in obliterating all traces of me from the house, convincing Saul that the place needed a 'fresh look', something to reflect his own personality that wouldn't harbor any sorrowful memories.

Yet somehow he managed to hang on to the slipper chair. I took comfort in that. At least there was one memory of me that Saul wanted to live with. I was proud of him for standing up to Mary Lynn on this. It also gave me hope.

I crossed to the chair and curled into the seat, hugging my knees to my chin. I rested my cheek on my knees and studied my sleeping husband. From this vantage point I could look at him to my heart's content. The big bed seemed oddly empty without Max and Ginger, whose habit had been to snuggle close to the warmth of Saul's body. I usually got up before anyone and it always made me smile to see the three of them bunched up together in the big bed. I missed that lumpy conglomeration of sleeping figures.

He lay on his back, as usual, a worried expression on his face. Most people look peaceful when they're sleeping, but not my Saul. Even in repose, his brows knitted together in a frown. Tonight it seemed more pronounced than usual, making him look downright cross.

A swell of tenderness washed over me. I unfolded myself from the chair and knelt beside the bed. With a butterfly's touch I tried to smooth out the puckers on his forehead. His head moved in response, but he didn't awaken. I rested a palm on his forehead. I closed my eyes and touched my lips to his hair.

I remained like this for several minutes, allowing my thoughts to transfer to his subconscious. I thought I should be reciting something, almost like casting a spell. I opted for the most mundane of mantras, reiterating *don't go...don't go...* Unoriginal, I know, but to the point. I was in no mood to waste time thinking up something more eloquent.

I conjured images of possible tragedies associated with the trip–plane crash, faulty bungee equipment, jeep going off the mountain road, poisonous spider bite–and transferred them to Saul's psyche. I sent images of him taking the fateful stride off the bungee platform, hurtling down and down until he reached the end of the cord's extension. At the moment of rebound, the cord snapped apart and Saul hit the rocky river at a speed that rendered the water as unforgiving as concrete.

His sleeping body spasmed once and his eyelids began to twitch, heralding the dream state. I retreated to the slipper chair and let the dream have its way.

His body remained still. The only evidence that my message got through was in the muted cooing sounds he made. I knew the projected scenes flitted through his brain with lightning speed. Strange how a single dream can seem to last all night when we're having it. Most people don't realize that multiple dreams take only seconds, even the harrowing ones that seem to go on forever and leave us to wake up exhausted. I didn't like disturbing Saul's peace of mind, but if this dream felt like an eight-hour nightmare, it was for his own good. I wanted him to hear what I had to say, loud and clear.

He got the message soon enough. He became restless, turning this way and that. He emitted a strangled yell that didn't come easily in sleep, more like the cry was being dragged from his throat. He shot upright in bed, full awakening taking a few seconds while his temporarily roving spirit re-entered the physical body. Disoriented, he looked around. He propped up the pillows against the headboard and leaned back, taking deep breaths until his heartbeat slowed to a normal pace. He threw back the covers and padded to the bathroom. I heard the faucet go on and off, and then the toilet flush. A moment later, he came back to bed, droplets of water still clinging to his face. He slid down between the sheets, and exhaled deeply.

I permitted myself a smug smile, certain that I had produced the desired effect. This turned out to be easier than I had expected. It was very gratifying to have solved my problem so quickly and neatly. And everyone told me not to get involved...

I blew him a kiss on my way out, confident that New Zealand would have to do without Saul McBride for the time being. I stopped short in front of the bedroom door. One look at the dresser told me the bridal photo was missing. I opened the top drawer on the side that had held my tee shirts. There it was, lying face-down atop a pair of satin boxer shorts that wasn't mine.

The realization that Saul had put away my picture weighed me down like a cement overcoat. All lightness fled and I fell to the floor, stung. Despite all the intimacy I'd witnessed between Saul and Mary Lynn, it never occurred to me that Saul might put away my picture. Had Mary Lynn asked him to do it, or did he not want any reminders of me while making love to another woman?

It's childish and I admit it, but I couldn't wait to come back the next evening to watch Saul put the kibosh on Mary Lynn's dream vacation. I made myself comfortable in the living room around six, impatient for them to return from work. It was almost nine o'clock before the door to the garage opened and I heard their voices in the kitchen.

"Whew, I'm stuffed," Saul said.

"The food is always wonderful at Martine's," Mary Lynn agreed.

Martine's was the upscale Italian restaurant Saul had taken me to on my thirtieth birthday, the one and only time we ever dined there. He used to say that we had to save it for very special occasions since it was so overpriced. Yet here he was, taking Mary Lynn there on an ordinary Monday night. Then again, maybe this *was* a special occasion. After all, tonight Mary Lynn would get shot down.

"...hope you understand, M.L.," Saul was saying.

"I am disappointed, darling, I won't lie to you. If you've made up your mind, then that's the way it is."

He did it! He told her the trip was off! I danced around the living room. He probably had broached it at dinner, after a cocktail and a nice Shiraz had mellowed her out. The success of my plan superseded any regret over personally not seeing the wind being taken out of Mary Lynn's sails.

Saul tossed his keys on the kitchen counter. "C'mon, M.L., you don't *really* mind flying coach instead of first-class, do you?"

"Well, it is an awfully long flight..." Mary Lynn pouted prettily, then circled her arms around Saul's waist. "But since you offered to upgrade the hotel room, I won't complain."

"That's my girl." He draped his arms over her shoulders. "See? We can save a little on airfare and still enjoy the lap of luxury."

"*Mmmm*. The suite may be so inviting we won't want to leave it long enough to do the bungee jump."

"Would that be so bad?"

Her body melted into his in a way that left no doubt as to her reply.

I banged my fists on the coffee table. I had been so sure the dream convinced Saul to forget this ludicrous undertaking.

Mary Lynn stopped kissing him long enough to ask, "You're not worried anymore about those meaningless premonitions you had last night?"

Saul eye-smiled down at her. "Nope. Now that you've explained that dreams don't directly represent what they appear to, I feel much better. In fact, I'd like to get a copy of that dream analysis book you mentioned."

"Don't bother, darling, you can borrow mine."

Either Mary Lynn was more masterful than I gave her credit for, or Saul had completely lost his mind.

I rehashed the previous night, trying to pinpoint where I had gone wrong. I hated to admit it, but Mary Lynn was correct in her assessment of dreams. The images and situations represented in the dream itself often have little to do with the real meaning behind them. I would have to come up with something a little meatier that would get Saul thinking.

In fact, as long as he planned to borrow M.L.'s dream analysis book, why not see how well he does his homework? If it's symbolism Saul needs, symbolism he'll get. There wasn't a brick wall I couldn't bounce back from. By the time I'm through with him, Mary Lynn will be lucky if he travels with her to the post office.

Chapter Eleven

Trying a symbolic dream on Saul when he was alone had to be the most sensible course, as I didn't want Mary Lynn around to distract him. Since they had fallen into a pattern of sleeping at their respective homes on Sunday nights, I waited until the next weekend before making a return trip to the house. All right, so the direct approach hadn't worked. I had nothing to lose by trying a little banal allegory, and this time no one would be there to tell him otherwise.

Late Sunday night I breezed into our bedroom, not bothering to tiptoe. Funny, Saul lay asleep on his side. As long as I could remember, he always slept flat on his back, but I suppose he had to change position some time. He faced away from the corner with the slipper chair, so I drifted to the other side of the bed where I could see his face. His worried forehead crinkled even more than before, but that was all good. If he already had something weighing on his mind, it might enhance the dream's impact.

I went to work.

Saul waited in line at a sidewalk produce stand, the kind found all over New York City. Brightly colored displays of fruits and vegetables stood under the awning, beckoning customers inside. People queued up for a special shipment of kiwi fruit that had just been delivered. Customers were limited to four kiwis per person, but clearly the long line proved that the grocers would run out before everyone had a chance to make their purchase.

The line progressed Soviet style: a grocer handed brown paper bags containing four kiwis to each customer in turn, who then moved to another line to pay. When Saul's turn came to pay, he handed the bag to the Korean woman at the cash register, who checked to make sure he had nothing other than kiwi fruit inside.

The cashier looked inside the bag, then looked at Saul. She didn't ring up the sale; she just stood there, looking at him.

"Is something wrong?" Saul asked.

"Must not eat these," she declared. "Poison."

Saul looked at the woman as if she had lost her mind. "I'm sure they're fine."

"No fine. Poison."

Patiently he asked, "If they are poisoned, why are you selling them to all these customers?"

"Theirs not poison. Only these." She held up Saul's paper bag.

Saul had waited half an hour in line for this? He counted to ten. "And what makes you so sure of this?" he asked the cashier.

"I know these things. I be here long time and I know."

Saul's patience reached its limit. "Thanks for the

warning, but I'm sure they're fine. Please just ring them up." He took out his wallet and counted out bills.

"You no buy these." The woman held the bag out of Saul's reach.

Saul cursed under his breath. He looked around the shop and called out. "Is the manager here?"

Mary Lynn emerged from a back room, a large ring of keys in her hand. She approached the cash register and snatched the bag of fruit from the cashier's hand. "I'm sorry, sir," she smiled winningly at Saul. "We've had a number of complaints about this cashier. I assure you she won't behave like this again." She handed the bag to Saul. "With my compliments, sir, for the inconvenience."

Saul murmured his thanks and replaced the money in his wallet, giving the manager an appraising look not lost on her. "Do come back and see me," she purred. Saul walked to the door, turned, and held out his hand to her. Without a moment's hesitation, Mary Lynn placed her key ring on top of the cash register and walked to the door. She took Saul's hand and they left the shop together. Once on the sidewalk, Mary Lynn took the bag of fruit from Saul. She reached inside and pulled out a kiwi, mysteriously peeled and sliced. She fed Saul a slice as if it were wedding cake and he tasted it with relish, licking the juice from his lower lip.

Mary Lynn watched with cool detachment as Saul's eyes grew wide and he began to cough. He tugged at the knot of his tie and pointed to his throat, struggling to draw breath. Mary Lynn stood there as he went down, strangling noises coming from deep inside his chest. People walked past, unseeing, uncaring.

The noises grew fainter after a minute or two, then stopped altogether and he grew still, eyes wide open and staring. Mary Lynn knelt down beside him and tenderly kissed his parted lips. In one deft movement, she removed his wallet from his pocket and stepped over his body to walk back inside the shop.

Saul's head thrashed back and forth on the pillow and he emitted soft straining sounds. No peaceful slumber this time. I smiled at this evidence of the dream's success, wondering how I could possibly contain myself for the few remaining hours until he awakened and phoned Mary Lynn to cancel the New Zealand trip. I settled into the slipper chair to wait.

When the alarm clock rang at seven-thirty the next morning, Saul rose in his usual cheery fashion. Never a morning person myself, this habit always made me envious and resentful. He never needed coffee to wake up, while I mainlined at least two strong cups before I felt remotely human. His mood had always been impossibly sunny while I was barely coherent. As he went whistling into the bathroom this morning, I slumped in the chair. He didn't seem the least bit unsettled by the dream.

I decided to tag along with him throughout the day, hoping later he'd reveal something to confirm that the dream had worked. But first I made a quick, necessary trip back to level Seven. I was scheduled to work at the Jungle that afternoon, so I asked Siobhan to take over my shift while I kept watch on my husband. She proved to be a real friend when she asked no questions, even though she knew I had just been with him. I was grateful for that. She always willingly helped me out when I needed her, even though she disapproved of what I was doing.

Following Saul from place to place wasn't easy. In order to do so, I had to keep myself in the astral plane, the one right next to the physical world. Because I wasn't supposed to be there anymore, it required a lot of spiritual energy to remain there for a sustained period of time. The impulse to drift back up to level Seven was powerful and I had to concentrate hard on staying put in that in-between realm. I was determined not to leave until I had found out what I needed to know.

At the office, at lunch, even during his workout at the gym, he said not a word about the dream. He didn't show any traces of anxiety. In fact, he seemed especially happy.

The long day of spiritual exertion had exhausted me, but I stuck to Saul like flypaper all day and into the evening, even while he picked up Mary Lynn for their dinner date. In my weariness I began to second-guess myself yet again. Saul was evidently happy. Was it right of me to put a damper on that happiness? Ashraf's voice echoed in my head: *Saul must be allowed to learn his own life lessons.* I returned my same argument: what good is spiritual existence if you can't help the souls you love?

By the time Saul and Mary Lynn came home from eating Chinese, I had reached the conclusion that I must have failed again. Saul had said not a word to Mary Lynn about the dream or the trip. Utterly spent and frustrated with my dual defeat, I dragged myself back to Seven to figure out my next move.

Figuring I could use a break, I spent the entire next day at the Jungle, rejuvenating myself with the animal souls I so loved. Watching their boundless energy and carefree affection helped restore some of my optimism. I wasn't about to give up on Saul. There had to be a way to get through to him before it was too late. I ached to bounce it all off Siobhan or Suse J, but knew better than to discuss it with them. No way would they give me an objective opinion.

I reviewed the two dreams over and over again, searching for a clue to why they had failed. Had I tried too hard? Elaborate schemes and symbols might have clouded the message I tried to send. It wasn't that Saul didn't listen to the dreams; he just couldn't really hear them. What would happen if I was just myself and told Saul exactly what I had on my mind? I had overlooked the simplest, most direct solution: rendezvous with Saul's spirit while he slept and spell out the dangers of New Zealand and the bungee excursion.

He wouldn't be sleeping alone that night, but no way could I wait until next Sunday to try again. The suspense was overpowering. Besides, time was running out on me.

If I didn't get through to him soon, he might very well forge ahead with the travel plans. This third time *had* to be the charm.

I went that night to his bedside and tried to ignore the satin-clad body next to his, blonde hair fanned out on the pillow. I knelt on the floor next to Saul's side of the bed and studied his face. Tonight the worried expression barely showed at all. If I hadn't known to look for it, I might not have noticed the slight wrinkle in his brow.

Taking a deep breath, I closed my eyes and silently spoke to the soul of my husband. I pictured him sitting up and looking at me, delighted and surprised at our reunion, holding his arms out to me. We embraced and I told him lovingly but firmly that he must *not* go on this trip to New Zealand. I gave no specifics this time, gave him no chance for rebuttals. I let the impetus of the message speak for itself. I thought of looking deep into his hazel eyes and concentrating my entire essence into a single thought: *do not go to New Zealand. Please, Saul, don't go. Please.*

Mary Lynn awoke the next morning before the alarm clock went off. She stretched and glanced at the sleeping Saul. Smiling, she pushed back her disheveled hair and touched his lips with her own. His eyelids crept open and he smiled back. She kissed him again, this time with more determination. His arms reached up to take her.

I groaned. Didn't they ever take a breather? I was in no mood today to tiptoe around Mary Lynn's sexual appetites, but there seemed to be no help for it. I'd better come back another time when they weren't likely to be screwing, if such a time existed. Just as I was about to leave, Saul's lingering languor disappeared and he came sharply awake. He pushed Mary Lynn away and sat upright. It was as though someone had dashed a bucket of cold water on him.

Mary Lynn sat back on her heels, the spaghetti strap of her nightgown sliding off one shoulder. "What's wrong?"

He raked a hand through his hair. Remnants of the previous evening's artfully gelled spikes stood out from his scalp. My, but Saul was getting hip...

"I had the weirdest dream."

She leaned forward to nuzzle his neck. "Was I in it?" she cooed.

He sat unresponsive to the caress and she drew back in displeasure. She considered her attentions above disregard.

"Do you want to talk about it?" It was a perfunctory question. She knew he expected her support, but she didn't bother to mask her disdain.

He turned to her, hurt and angry. "I wouldn't *think* of boring you." He threw back the covers and swung his legs over the side of the bed, turning his back to her.

Good for you, Saul!

Mary Lynn immediately changed tactics. "Darling, you're upset." She caressed his back. "Please tell me about it. I want to help."

Saul unbent a little at the apologetic approach. He swiveled his neck to look her in the eye. "It was about

Judith. You sure you still want to hear it?"

Only another woman could have detected the slight stiffening in Mary Lynn's posture. It was glaring to me that she wanted to hear nothing of the sort, but she couldn't very well admit that to him.

She cast her eyes down in her best affronted manner. "You must think me a very small person to be jealous of your wife's memory, Saul. Judith was my friend, too."

Saul backpedaled so fast he almost achieved lift-off. "Of course she was," he said, remorse coating every syllable. "That was tactless of me. I forget how much you miss her, too."

Give me a break!

Mary Lynn kneed her way closer and began kneading his shoulders. "Tell me about the dream, darling."

Saul closed his eyes as he relaxed under her massaging hands. *Judith who?*

"It was so strange...Judith was just there, talking to me."
"Where?"

"Right next to the bed. There was a kind of blackness all around her, like a photography backdrop. She looked great...radiant, in fact."

Mary Lynn's eyes narrowed.

"She had on that blue suit, the one we buried her in. She always looked so gorgeous in that. Ouch! Not so hard, M.L."

"Sorry. Go on."

"Anyway, she just stood there like she presided over a

shareholders' meeting or something. I heard her voice, clear as day. She kept saying, 'Don't do it, Saul. Don't do it.' She just kept repeating that over and over." He turned around to face Mary Lynn. "I think she may have been telling me not to take the New Zealand trip."

Mary Lynn's laughter tinkled in the stillness of the room. "Oh, Saul. I never figured you to be superstitious."

"I'm not talking about a rabbit's foot or four-leaf clover, here. She *spoke* to me, Mary Lynn. It was so distinct, I can hear it even now."

Neither of them said anything for a moment. Mary Lynn's shoulders were hunched with tension. I could see her weighing the best technique to use at this juncture.

Saul broke the silence. "Why don't we just go to Las Vegas instead? You've been wanting to stay at the Bellagio."

Mary Lynn cleared her throat. "I was thinking of Vegas more along the lines of a honeymoon spot, not a consolation trip."

Honeymoon?

"Oh, I can think of better places for a honeymoon than the Strip," Saul teased. "How does Fiji strike you?"

"It sounds heavenly, but I *really* want to try bungee jumping in Queenstown first."

It was then that I recognized the truth about Mary Lynn. She had never been our friend, never had our best interests at heart. She didn't even have real feelings for Saul. She had feelings for his money. And she wanted to get her hands on it as Mrs. McBride. I don't know why it took me this long to see it.

Mary Lynn straightened Saul's shoulders and resumed massaging them. "Darling, you're much too intelligent to believe in nonsense like dreams and omens. It's only natural that a widower should dream of his wife." She nestled her chin in the space between his neck and shoulder, crossing her arm over his chest. "This isn't some lame attempt to get out of our trip, now is it?" She nibbled on his earlobe. "People jump this site all the time. It's perfectly safe. And everything's all planned." She drew her fingertips lightly over his bare chest. "I wouldn't put you in harm's way, darling. You believe that, don't you?"

Saul gave a muted groan as her fingers circled his nipple. There could be no question of the powerful effect this woman had on him. He couldn't deny her much.

"Say we can go, Saul," Mary Lynn breathed. "You know how much this trip means to me."

Saul's answer was to reach behind him and pull her into his arms. He kissed her savagely and pressed her shoulders down on the bed. She seemed to welcome the assertiveness and wrapped her long limbs around his body in a gesture of complete possession.

I knew then I had lost him.

Chapter Twelve

I wasn't used to the feeling of helplessness that consumed me after that night. I was accustomed to making things happen. Which is not the same as getting your way all the time, or getting things handed to you on a silver platter whenever you crook a finger. If I wanted something badly enough, I worked for it. This time had been no different...except that I seemed to be *less* powerful as a discarnate spirit than I had been as a mere mortal. The most frustrating part was that I had failed to arouse Saul's better judgment all because Mary Lynn never failed to arouse other parts of him.

If ever I needed a shoulder to cry on, it was now. I could have really used Ashraf's advice, but I wasn't in the mood for the lecture he would inevitably give. Siobhan and Suse J were both at work, and there was only one other soul who knew about my little intrigue.

Justin was hanging out in his front yard when he saw me striding toward him. He came forward to meet me, making me halt in mid-step. He'd never done that before. Far from being pleasantly surprised, the improvement in his manners set off some distant warning bells. In my vulnerable frame of mind, level Four was not someplace I wanted to be, but right now I needed to talk and Justin was the only confidante available.

He came closer, his snide expression even more pronounced today than usual. I told myself it was an attempt to mask his pleasure at my visit. Expressing true emotion seemed to be something Justin Caso avoided at all costs.

He stopped a good two feet away and gave me a hard look. "You did it, dint you." It was not a question.

I thought about using the *I don't know what you're talking about* approach, but why pretend? "You'll be glad to know it didn't work," I retorted. "He didn't get the message."

"I told ya."

"You did not," I countered childishly. "You only told me not to attempt it. You couldn't have known Mary Lynn would…distract him."

"Just as well."

Before I had a chance to ask what he meant, Justin grabbed my arm and pulled me alongside him. "C'mon, Ms. J. We're gonna take a li'l road trip."

I twisted my arm out of his grip. "Don't grab me. Where I come from, friends respect each other, you know?"

He answered with a surly look. Why was he so angry with me?

"Just trust me for once, okay? I got something I wanna show you." He didn't touch me; this time he held out his hand. I glanced at his fingernails rimmed with black.

The idea of going with him somewhere didn't thrill me, but curiosity won out. Whatever he wanted to show me might explain his stranger-than-usual behavior. Besides, maybe he would show me something that would help me stop Saul. "All right then, I'll go. But wherever we're going, I can't stay long." I gingerly put my hand in his grimy one, happy to close my eyes in preparation for the mystery trip.

They were still closed when the reek of methane and sulphur, like standing in a pit of manure and rotten eggs, assaulted my nose. It didn't compromise my breathing, of course, but I perceived the stench just as intensely as I would have back on earth. I squinted my eyes open a mere crack, afraid they might start watering.

The air, thick and steamy as August in Alabama, made gooseflesh rise on my arms. I rubbed them briskly. I had no physiological need to perspire, but I felt the discomfort as though sticky sweat covered my body. I peered around in the dim light, trying to focus. I looked up at the sky for the sun, but it was completely dark. No planets or stars, no glowing comet tails, just inky, empty black.

I looked at Justin, and curled my lip at him for bringing me someplace so dismal. He nodded, but seemed oblivious to the stink and gloom. He probably had been here before and knew what to expect, he was so blasé. He actually seemed comfortable in this hole.

He took hold of my elbow, gently, and steered me forward, but I locked my feet in place.

"We're not going a step farther until you tell me what this is all about." I had to shout over the pervasive din that sounded like the world's largest radiator, a loud, droning hiss that pummeled my head.

"All high and mighty, huh?" he bellowed over the noise. "Okay, I'll tell you. Since I can't get through to you with common sense, you need a little demonstration. I'm gonna show you what's in store for you if you keep on with this shit-brained plan of yours to rescue your old man."

He swept his arm in display, like Vanna White presenting a brand-new Lincoln Navigator. "Welcome to level One, Ms. J. The lowest rung on the ladder. You've heard about it. Sometimes it's called 'hell.'"

My face registered what he looked for. Shocked, yes, but not as frightened as he would have liked. I didn't let fear take hold of me; I was only passing through. In fact, now that I knew where I was, why the fetid smell and the irksome racket, I wanted to see more. Was there really fire and brimstone? Where was the devil with the pointy tail?

Justin took advantage of the chink in my stubbornness. "C'mon." He lifted his chin in the direction he wanted to go.

I took a step, but almost fell flat. My torso had gone forward, but my legs didn't follow. I looked down at my feet and saw that they were mired in some kind of sticky muck that resembled mud and smelled like hot garbage. Considering our location, it was probably something much, much worse. I struggled to pick up my right leg. The tenacious glop made a loud sucking noise and stretched thin, refusing to let go of my shoe. I'd stumbled into a scene from *The Blob*, only Steve McQueen wasn't here to rescue me.

The trapped feeling of being stuck closed in on me. "Get this stuff off me!"

Justin bent down and held my foot steady with one hand while using his other hand to tug at the offending stuff, grunting with the effort. "Keep pulling your foot up."

Shoe and glop finally wrenched apart, but the momentum caused me to lose my balance. My arms flailed about in broad circles as I fought to stay upright. Justin grabbed my arms to steady me and held them there until I found my center of gravity. He pointed to a drier spot nearby. "Here, put your foot down here while I get the other one loose."

I held on to his shoulder while we pulled my other foot clear. Both feet now on drier ground, I alternated knee lifts, relieved to be ambulatory and feeling sheepish for having almost panicked.

I hurried Justin away and we picked our way along a landscape as barren as the moon's surface. I'm not sure you could even call it landscape, just an endless expanse of shit-muck that clung to my shoes and stunk up my world. An unwelcome sensation of heaviness engulfed me, just like at my funeral and the first time I saw Saul and Mary Lynn together. They were one-pound hand weights compared to the massive barbells I pressed now.

The realization that some souls were actually ensconced

here on a permanent basis hit me with a smothery *whonk*. They languished at the bottom of a deep, dark well. They could see a small circle of light at the top, but it was too far to reach. Their entire existence was reduced to this miserable, brown, lifeless wasteland. Smog pushed down on my lungs which made breathing a chore, and anxiety came back with a vengeance to claim me. There was no question of fight or flee. It was definitely flee.

When Justin saw that I might bolt at any moment, he seized my arm. "Nothing doing, Ms. J," he belted out above the noise. "Not 'til you seen some more." His grip was like an iron band, but I was too busy fighting my own panic to protest. Of the two evils, Justin manhandling me and finding myself in hell, Justin's mauling was the lesser.

He dragged me along the steamy flatlands until we spotted some crude, dilapidated shacks. Oily resin rivulets oozed down the exterior of the rough boards, drying in hard beads. No one was in sight, probably a good thing since the shacks clearly looked uninhabitable. I didn't even hear any signs of life. No voices, no barking dogs, or singing birds, just the unending discordant noise they had in movies about Vietnam POW camps that deprived the prisoners of sleep.

Each time we sidestepped the occasional pool of vomit, I wanted to gag. Any initial curiosity I had about hell had given way to alarm and had now rapidly turned into revulsion. This must have been where Ash had referred to at my orientation when he said that Hitler was spending his time somewhere very unpleasant. I had no idea, on that long-ago day, what an understatement he had made.

Without warning, the pitiless rank odor intensified, and I couldn't stifle a gag. Justin eyed me smugly. "Whatsa matter, Ms. J? Dontcha like it down here?"

Breathing any more of that putrid smell was out of the question, but I couldn't speak without breathing. I wasn't about to let Justin's behavior go unchecked. I braced myself and said, "What I don't like is your interminable sarcasm."

"Yeah? There's a lot you don't like. But you better get used to it 'cuz this is where you're gonna end up if you keep scammin' like you are."

"I don't know what you're talking about." Imperious.

"The hell you don't. You know exactly what I'm talking about. You just don't wanna hear it, especially from me."

I refused to admit to myself that there might be some truth in Justin's pontifications. I certainly wasn't about to admit it to him.

I lifted my chin. "Are you finished?"

"Hell, no, I ain't finished."

"Well, I am." Without another word, I spun around and closed my eyes to teleport home. I couldn't wait to get out of there.

I opened them and saw that I had come back to Justin's front yard on level Four; an unexpected diversion from my flight plan, but not unwelcome. I was so glad to be away from level One, I didn't care where I ended up. In fact, the sparse, withered weeds of Justin's yard never looked more glorious. What had previously been an eyesore was now a sight for sore eyes.

It was reassuring to see signs of life, such as they were on Four. The colors may have been drab, but they were *colors*. The sky might be perpetually overcast, but it contained light. And the air...I took a deep breath of stale, stuffy air that seemed like intoxicating perfume.

I giggled in sheer relief. If I felt like this about level Four, my own level would really feel like heaven.

A draft of hot, moist air against the back of my neck shattered the euphoria. I whirled around and came face to face with Justin. He stood with one knee cocked and a menacing look on his face that raised my hackles.

Just then, he lunged. Grasping my shoulders with both hands, he burrowed his mouth into my neck like a determined rodent, biting, sucking. It happened so fast I didn't have time to panic, just to react. With all the force I could muster, I pushed him away and stood poised to run. Our eyes locked on each other like two pit bulls about to do battle.

If I had veins, adrenalin would have been pumping through them like mad. This wasn't my unlikely friend Justin Caso standing with his hands casually stuffed into those deep pockets of his, but a spirit strange to me, one who frightened me.

His snide smirk reappeared as he stared at me, tinged with a leer that put my defenses on red alert. Before I could think of what my next move should be, he lunged again, locking his arms around me. Immobilized, I strained my face away from his streaked, whitish tongue that followed my evasions with the persistence of a bloodhound. I pushed against him with all my might, but he didn't budge.

He grabbed my breast and squeezed hard. "You really get to me, Ms. J," he muttered. "Always did." I struggled harder, which only made him laugh. "Don't go acting all indignant. Discarnate spirits get horny, too, you know."

I forced myself to speak with a calm I really didn't feel. "No, they don't. Sexual cravings belong only to physical bodies."

"Maybe on Seven, but not here. Whaddya think I'm down here for? That's part of the karma I gotta work out. We'll just call this a little 'f-o-u-r' play." He chuckled at his own wit and forced my arm upwards behind my back, pressing me even closer until his mouth almost touched mine, his breath sour on my face. "Let's face it. We both know you don't really belong up There."

I tried to stall. "Don't I?"

"Not with the schemes you dream up. The way I see it, you ain't so far along in your soul growth as you like to think. Otherwise, you wouldn't be messing in other people's lives." He ground his pelvis against mine. "You belong down here with me. Shit, I'll even let you redecorate." He chuckled and buried his mouth in my neck.

Fast losing any control over the situation, I had to do something before Justin completely lost his sense of reason. God knows what he was capable of doing.

Still imprisoned in his grasp, I acted haughty. "Justin Caso, this has gone far enough. Let me loose right now. I'm leaving."

"You think you're leaving, but you ain't. You ain't going back up There."

"Go to hell," I spat.

He roared with laughter. "Lady, I'm already more than halfway there."

Now I was downright scared. This was like some demented bodice-ripping novel gone awry, and the implications terrified me. If Justin was serious about keeping me here with him on level Four, no one on Seven would know where to look for me. Even if they did, I doubted anyone would jeopardize his own soul growth by rescuing me from a self-inflicted mistake. Not after they all warned me not to get involved.

Not knowing what else to do, I made a desperate attempt to teleport myself out of his hold. I squeezed my eyes shut and tried to focus on level Seven. *Please, please, let me be back home.*

When I opened them, I still stood locked in Justin's grip. In my panic I had been trying too hard and couldn't muster enough spiritual energy. His slitty eyes looked dangerous and I braced myself for what might come next.

As abruptly as he had attacked me, he now released me. I stared at him, wondering what he had up his sleeve, but he just stood there as casually as if he waited for a bus, one knee at that rakish angle. He took out a cigarette. *Was it good for you?*

I didn't waste any more time wondering what he was up to. I took advantage of this momentary freedom and tried for home again. I took a couple of deep, calming breaths and closed my eyes, more softly this time. I pictured my light-filled house on Seven, mentally sniffing the potted hyacinths on the kitchen windowsill. The tension began to melt away and I was confident that in a second or two I would be out of this mess and back in my comfort zone. I smiled with anticipation of home and opened my eyes.

The smile quickly faded.

My foiled efforts amused Justin. "It's no good, Ms. J. I guess your flight's been cancelled."

I just glared at him.

"Aw, dint anyone tell you?" he asked with feigned sympathy. "You'd think those spirit guides of yours woulda educated you better."

"Tell me what?" I gritted out.

"See, when souls absorb too much negative energy, it messes up the transportation. Maybe you been hanging around the wrong people lately." He slicked back a hank of oily hair that had fallen over his forehead and grappled in his pocket for another smoke.

I kept my eyes fixed on him, unsure of his next move, unsure of my own. Instinct screamed at me to run, but I feared it would only goad him to chase me down. If I could only calm myself down enough to get home…

Justin threw the half-smoked cigarette to the ground,

not bothering to stamp it out. We both watched it roll away into an oily puddle where it sizzled itself out. Silence hung heavy between us.

"You'll be back, Ms. J. You think this is the end, but it ain't. You'll be back." He shoved his hands into his jacket pockets and turned away. Whistling, he walked back to his house and disappeared inside.

When his front door creaked shut, I heaved a sigh of relief. Not wasting another second, I closed my eyes and concentrated on level Seven as I never have before. Shaken as I was by the ordeal, it took me a few minutes to get anywhere.

A sharp rapping sound from behind intruded on my concentration. I looked over my shoulder at the front window of Justin's house. He'd been watching me. He gave a jaunty wave and called from to me from inside, the irregular glass panes muffling his voice. "See ya around, Ms. J. Yeah, I'll be seein' ya."

Impotent rage replaced fear and I sucked air through my teeth. He began laughing as I closed my eyes again.

His laughter followed me all the way home.

I opened my eyes and found myself in front of the library on Seven, not caring one iota that I had landed short of my own house. All that mattered was that I had arrived safely back on my own level. Now if I could just get home. I put my head down as though I bucked a violent wind, not wanting to see anyone this strange afternoon.

Someone behind me called my name.

"Shit," I muttered, in no mood to see anyone. Reluctantly I turned around. Suse J waved at me from the library steps. I pointed at the air in front of me, pantomiming that I had an urgent appointment. I had no desire to talk to anyone just now, least of all her. She wasn't easy to fool and I had no intention of confessing my disturbing encounter with Justin. Thankfully, she picked up on my charade and waved me on, but I felt her eyes boring into my back as I went.

In the sanctuary of my kitchen, I set a pot of chamomile tea to steep and sat down to think. Today's events were all the convincing I needed to distance myself from Justin, but that meant losing my only real confidante in the Saul situation. Confiding in Siobhan or Suse J might be safer, but I knew their opinions about my plans regarding Saul. Neither they nor anyone else up Here would support me in this. Not that I needed anyone's blessing to intervene on my husband's behalf, but a little moral support would have helped. I gave a deep sigh.

Nope, I was in this alone. And that was all right because ultimately it had to be my choice, my responsibility. I would draw solely from my own strength from here on out and not rely on anyone else. For good or ill, I was on my own.

Chapter Thirteen

Time was running out on me. The warning dreams I gave Saul put the proverbial bee in his bonnet, but Mary Lynn had succeeded in tossing the entire hat out the window. The bungee jumping trip was now three weeks away.

I turned to the person I had always relied on when I got into trouble.

Micaela would give him the message. He would listen to her, and Mary Lynn would have no reason to disabuse him of Mic's advice.

Ash had explained to me that an out-of-body experience is a common means of communication between spirits and their earthbound loved ones.

"Most people do not regard dreams in this context, but with the appropriate attitudes it can be a most useful mode of interface between the two worlds," he'd said.

"You mean sleeping people dream they are out of their bodies?"

"They do not just dream it; they *are* out of the bodies. A soul temporarily leaves his or her physical body during the dream state. It is connected to the body by a thick cord that prevents the spirit from drifting too far away from itself. Prior to awakening, spirit and cord disappear back into the physical body. The silver cord is never severed except at the end of earthly life, allowing the soul to leave the physical world and return to its home up Here."

I'd pondered this. "But that didn't happen when I visited Saul while he slept."

Ash had shrugged. "I cannot explain why."

My spirit guide without an answer? "Ash, I thought you possessed all the wisdom of the ages."

He'd smiled, but said nothing more.

So far, my luck with nocturnal communications had been less than stellar. I had no choice but to try again with Micaela. It would have been so much easier if I could have picked up the phone or sent her an email, but my spiritual abilities didn't stretch that far. Yet. Besides, how freaky would *that* be, getting an email from a dead friend? Micaela was a scientist. She'd never believe it might really be from me. She would chalk it up to someone's tasteless idea of a joke.

I wondered if she still had my phone number on speed-dial. She might hit that button by accident and hear my voice on the other end, but such fantasies were of little use. I didn't have a physical voice anymore and I wasn't able to project my spiritual energies into one that the human ear could detect. Even if I could, she still wouldn't believe it.

So it was the dream route or nothing, but first I would pay her a preliminary call to reconnect our souls. That might have been where I went wrong with Saul's dreams. I had assumed the connection between my husband and me still existed, as strong as ever. The connection was there, all right, but it couldn't handle the dreams I sent. I should have prepared him for the shock of hearing from me. If I contacted Micaela in advance, sent her a spiritual Save the Date card, the results might be better. It seemed worth a try.

When I arrived at the Pressmans' the next night, Micaela and Gerry were both sound asleep. Gerry lay on his stomach, one arm thrown protectively over his wife's supine figure. I sat on the foot rail of their California king size bed and studied Micaela, thinking back to all the special times we shared. So much of our earthly lives had been spent in a very special bond, one that I prayed would bear up under the burden I planned to impose.

A tiny smile crossed her sleeping face and I wondered if she, too, reminisced about us. I smiled back, though she couldn't see it. As I sat watching her, a spectral replicate of Micaela rose from her body, like she sat up and lay down at the same time. The spectral Micaela floated out from the top of the physical Micaela's head, rising until she was even with my perch on the bed rail.

We stared at each other in amazement, then looked down with equal amazement at the physical body, still asleep.

I stretched out a hand to her spiritual form. "Mic."

She extended her hand to clasp mine but stopped short as if the limits of her mobility were hampered by a tether. We both glanced down and saw what looked like a thick steel cable attached at mid-torso, anchoring Micaela's spirit body to the sleeping figure in the bed. Ashraf's explanation that dreams are literally out-of-body experiences was clearly demonstrated.

I wondered again why I hadn't seen this silver cord when I visited dreams upon Saul. Ah, but I hadn't really been interacting with him then. I had been on a mission, trying to get a message through to him, not communicating with him on an intimate level like this. At least, that's what I told myself. I much preferred this explanation to the one in the back of my mind. The one that said I hadn't seen the silver cord because Saul's spiritual connection with me wasn't at all as strong as I thought.

All this whisked through my brain as I sat looking at Micaela. I reached out to see what the cord felt like, but my hand passed right through it. It stood to reason that the cord connecting spirit and body was nothing to be tampered with.

Micaela continued to stare back at me, her mouth opening and closing, trying to speak and frustrated that she couldn't. Without warning the silver cord buckled and Micaela's spirit melted back into her sleeping body. We'd barely had a moment to interact, but we had actually made contact. My spirits rose to think that this time I had a very real chance to warn Saul about his misbegotten trip. I decided to send Micaela a dream and she would tell Saul not to go to New Zealand.

My dry run had been so promising that I couldn't wait for the all-important visit. I showed up at her house early the following night, a little after ten-thirty. She lay in bed still awake, reclining on a study pillow with a crossword puzzle against her upraised knees. Gerry, already asleep, snored with the soft rhythm of the contented. I offered a silent thank-you that they hadn't chosen this night for one of their rare nocturnal lovemaking sessions. Micaela once confided that their busy schedules usually limited their sex life to afternoon delight on weekends, but every so often they'd stir things up with evening activity. Lucky for me, tonight wasn't the night. I got enough of that with Saul and Mary Lynn.

Forty-five agonizing minutes later, Micaela laid the almost completed puzzle on the nightstand and switched off the bedside lamp. I sat motionless on my roost at the foot of the bed, waiting. The room was quiet save for Gerry's snores, which had dwindled to raspy breaths.

Something moved in my peripheral vision. I looked at my friend and watched the now-familiar sight of concurrent Micaelas: one in repose, one rising above, the silvery cord attached to both of them, longer than it had been last night. Spectral Micaela bobbed gently up and down as she floated in a kneeling position above her body, near the head of the bed.

In contrast to her surprised, almost panicky expression of the night before, she wore a serene look, not at all surprised to see me sitting on the end of her bed.

"Judith! How, uh...how are you?" What did one say in situations like this?

"Not bad for a dead woman," I quipped. Then, "Oh, Mic, it's amazing up Here. There's a kind of love that defies imagination."

To my dismay, she began to sob. There were no tears, but the anguish was real. "Jude, I've missed you so much. I couldn't help feeling somehow responsible..."

"Now see here, Dr. Pressman! You know full well my death was a fluke that couldn't be helped. You weren't the doctor in charge, remember."

Her mouth flattened in a thin smile. "I know. Gerry and Saul keep telling me the same thing." The smile faded. "Jude, about Saul–"

"You don't have to tell me, Mic. I've seen for myself what Saul's become."

"Then you know about Mary Lynn."

"Yes. That's why I need your help."

I explained to Micaela about the bungee jumping trip and why Saul mustn't go, how I had tried to warn him myself and failed.

"...and it's not that I can predict the future or anything. It's just a gut feeling I have that's too strong to ignore. I can't explain it, not even to myself. I just know that if Saul takes this trip, it will be his last. I can't let that happen."

Micaela listened and nodded in sympathy. "I knew they planned to go bungee jumping, but I didn't realize they were going to New Zealand to do it. But Jude, why do you believe Saul will die on *this* trip? You said yourself that you can't predict the future."

"I wish I could give you a valid explanation. I just *know* it, as surely as I know that I'm sitting here talking to you." I reached for her hand. She clasped it, unhampered this time by the silver cord. "Please, Micaela, don't let him go through with it."

She squeezed my hand. "Jude, my Judith. You know I'll help you in any way I can. But if Saul didn't listen to you, what makes you so sure he's going to listen to me?"

"I'm not sure at all. But we have to try. You're more of an objective bystander, and without Mary Lynn's influence..."

Her face fell. "Objective bystander? Is that what I am?"

I could have kicked myself. "I'm sorry, sweetie. I didn't mean it that way. Of course you're more than just an outside observer to us. I only meant that the message will have greater impetus if it comes from someone other than me."

"Oh, sure. 'Saul, guess what? I had a long talk with Judith last night and she isn't too keen on your vacation plans.' Who wouldn't believe that?"

"You aren't even going to remember that we talked like this. You'll only have an ominous dream to tell him about."

She didn't look convinced. "I don't know...but if you say so..."

I covered our clasped hands with my free one. "Thank you, sweetie. And Mic, even if this doesn't work, thank you for being there–even though I'm up Here."

She grinned at the muddling syntax. "I love you, Judith. You know I'll do what I can."

"I love you, too, Mic."

Her image began to fade as the silver lifeline guided her spirit back into its body. Whether it was timed that way by a higher power or just serendipity that we wrapped things up when we did, I'll never know for certain.

Micaela slept peacefully. Gerry had even stopped snoring.

The next morning I hurried back to Micaela's to see what kind of impression my nocturnal visit had made. Gerry had an early surgery scheduled and had already left, but Micaela was still in bed, awake and staring at the ceiling with her hands folded under her head. The minute I saw her face, I knew we were getting somewhere. She had the same thoughtful but determined look she used to have in high school when we studied for exams.

The alarm clock went off, but she didn't get out of bed. She silenced the buzzer and sat up, drawing blanketed knees to her chest and clasping her hands around them. She sat like that for a minute, staring into space. Then her shoulders shimmied as though a cold draft had hit her, and she rubbed her arms.

The light furrow in her brow deepened. I regretted causing her uneasiness, but I knew it was for a good reason and only temporary. I would send her the dream tonight, and by tomorrow the deed would be done.

I hoped...

I knew Micaela well enough to tell when the wheels of her mind were turning. Already she thought of calling Saul. I might not even need to send her that dream.

The bedside clock illuminated seven-thirty, an early but not ungodly hour to phone somebody. I clapped my hands together in glee like a little child pleased with a puppet show.

Micaela rolled to Gerry's empty side of the bed and reached for the phone on his nightstand. She touched the speed-dial button, and the number for Saul's house, er, my house, our house connected with a rapid series of tones. I brought a hand to my heart: she *did* keep my number on speed dial. My sight suddenly became misty.

After two rings, Mary Lynn's sleepy voice answered. "Hello?"

If ever I was grateful for the perks of the afterlife, this was it. Like the picture-in-picture feature of a hi-def TV, the image of Mary Lynn on the other end of the phone appeared to me in the upper corner of Micaela's bedroom. Now I could hear and see both sides of the conversation.

Micaela hesitated. "May I please speak to Saul?"

On the other end of the phone, quiescence turned to annoyance. "Who is this?" The set of her jaw said that Mary Lynn knew exactly who it was.

"It's Micaela Pressman, Mary Lynn. May I talk to Saul, please? It's important."

Mary Lynn glanced over at Saul, still asleep next to her.

Satisfied that the ringing phone hadn't penetrated his slumber, she slid out of bed and took the portable handset into the bathroom, easing the door closed.

Micaela's voice emanated from the phone. "Hello? Mary Lynn, are you there?"

"What do you want, Micaela?" Mary Lynn hissed. "It's awfully early to be disturbing people with phone calls."

Micaela bristled. "It's not too early for people who go to work for a living."

Well done, Mic! My friend apparently had developed some chops during my absence from earth. Quick comebacks had never been Micaela's long suit, so I was proud of her. Unfortunately, the barb was a futile one: Mary Lynn's accounting practice was thriving. Don't ask me how, with all the traveling she did.

"Is Saul there or not?"

"Not," Mary Lynn shot back. "He's left for work already."

As far back as anyone could remember, Saul had never left for work before nine o'clock. He said it was his one rebellion against the establishment. Of course, he never acknowledged the fact that he compensated by staying at the office until six. He still thought he had achieved a *coup*.

Micaela decided to gamble on Mary Lynn's feelings for Saul. "Mary Lynn, listen to me. I'm talking to you not as Judith's friend, but as Saul's. I'm asking you two not to go to New Zealand."

"Why shouldn't we?"

Micaela knew how implausible her reason would have sounded to even a sympathetic listener. She was sure Mary Lynn would hang up when she heard what Micaela had to say, but she forged ahead anyway. "I had a terrible dream last night. I dreamed that Saul would die on this trip."

Mary Lynn didn't hang up, but her laugh was scornful. "Oh, please. Did you perhaps have a little too much to drink last night?"

"I didn't drink at all last night. I'm serious about this."

"You've been watching too much television, Micaela. Don't you know that the chances are greater of being struck by lightning than dying in a plane crash?"

"It's not the plane I'm worried about."

"What, then?"

"Well, it *could* be a plane crash...I mean...I'm not really sure how or when he would die; I just know it will happen if you go to New Zealand. You probably won't believe this, Mary Lynn, but Judith came to me in this dream and told me that Saul must not take this trip. When I woke up this morning, the feeling was so powerful, I couldn't ignore it. Saul needs to know."

Mary Lynn was quiet for a moment. "Well, well, what do you know. Judith was in your dream."

"Mary Lynn, please. This isn't about Judith. This is about Saul. If you really care for him, you'll give it some thought."

There was silence on both ends of the phone. Micaela held her breath. So did I.

Mary Lynn became solicitous. "Well, Micaela, this is certainly an unexpected turn of events. I'll tell you what let's do. Why don't you take your paranormal bullshit and go...straight...to hell." Had she shouted the last four words, they couldn't have been more biting.

"I know how crazy this sounds, but–"

"Do you? Do you know how crazy this sounds? I don't think so, Micaela. I think you have a thing for Saul and you're just pissed off that you never got a crack at him. I think you'll use any excuse to keep him from being happy with me."

Telltale stirrings in the bed came from the other side of the bathroom door and Mary Lynn quickly ended the conversation. "Thanks *awfully* for your concern, Micaela. I'll be sure to let Saul know you called to wish us *bon voyage*."

The click in Micaela's ear gave her no chance to reply. At the same time, the picture-in-picture of Mary Lynn popped like a soap bubble. Micaela hung up the phone and massaged her temples. I didn't have to be clairvoyant to know why her head throbbed. What I didn't know yet was that her headache sprang from something more than just dealing with Mary Lynn.

She climbed out of bed and padded to the bathroom. Her face was ashy but it didn't mask the determination still etched on it. Thank God, she wasn't going to give up. If I knew Micaela, she planned to talk to Saul in person. He might not accept her explanation, but at least he would hear her out.

I took a deep breath. It was going to be a long day for both of us.

Correction: for all of us.

Chapter Fourteen

As a member of the cardiology staff at B'nai Brith Hospital, Micaela's workdays were hectic. This afternoon had been no exception. In addition to making her rounds of post-op patients, she was paged to the ER for an MI, STAT. Then one of her bypass patients coded and–well, you get the idea.

It was after seven in the evening by the time Micaela made her way to the hospital garage where she parked her Altima. Dusk was deepening and it had grown colder than usual for early April. Micaela swiped her parking pass through the automatic attendant and the exit's barrier arm rose. The car emerged from the garage into a steady drizzle of sleet that had been only an afternoon sprinkle when she last saw daylight.

The Altima's windshield turned into a screen of fog as the rain pick-a-picked at the glass. She didn't realize the weather had turned so dismal. She also didn't realize I rode shotgun with her.

Apparently still consumed with the memory of the morning's conversation with Mary Lynn, Mic seemed to be functioning on autopilot. She switched on the defogger and windshield wipers with mechanical movements that told me her thoughts were miles away, probably somewhere with Saul. I knew she wouldn't waste any time going to see him about my warning. What would she say to him? How would she stress the importance of the dream without sounding like an hysteric?

The heaviest of rush-hour traffic was over, but a good many vehicles still clogged the city streets. It took two cycles of traffic light changes before Micaela could make her way across the next major intersection. Cars tailgated, horns honked, and sleet continued to fall. Why did inclement weather always bring out the latent hostility in drivers?

The Altima crept toward the intersection. Michaela crossed her fingers, hoping the stale green light would remain green just a few seconds longer. If she could ease into the intersection before the light turned red, at least she could justify her presence there to the angry, gridlocked traffic and not have to wait through another light cycle.

She inched closer to the bright green glow. The rear lights on the car in front of her flashed a brighter red, prompting her to tap her own brakes. She glanced at the dashboard clock and turned up the defogger fan a notch. When she raised her eyes again, the car ahead of her had made it to the other side of the intersection. In those few seconds, the traffic light had turned yellow. I waited to see if Micaela might make a run for it. She was so scrupulous; never mind that people ran yellow lights all the time.

Micaela stole forward until the Altima lined up with the

semaphore, then braked to a halt. Damn her good-driver sensibilities. Saul's safety was at stake, and she drove as though she were in high school driver's ed class: *What do you do at a yellow light? Stop if safe to do so.*

The light stayed red for an eternity. Regretting her own ethics, Micaela berated herself under her breath. When the light turned green again, she confidently applied the accelerator. No pussyfooting around this time.

My next thought was that the Altima's mechanical systems must have gone berserk. One second Olivia Newton-John was belting out *let's get physical, physical* and the next second her voice slowed down like a Victrola in need of cranking. Tires screeched as the car spun around and Micaela braced her hand against the upholstered roof. Everything seemed to happen in slow motion as the car rotated several more times, stopping only when a street light pole smashed against the windshield, sending a shower of glass in all directions. The glare of the city lights, intensified by the rain, exploded at us like some crazy carnival. A belated, sickening crunch, and Micaela knew only blackness.

The SUV that broadsided us stood about ten feet away, only a crumpled grille marking its part in the accident. I wasn't hurt, of course, but poor Micaela was in bad shape. My reactions fluctuated between guilt and exoneration. It was my fault: if she hadn't been on her way to see Saul, this wouldn't have happened. It wasn't my fault: even if she hadn't been going to Saul's, she would have been driving home under the same road conditions.

How I wanted to be there for her, as she had always been for me! I wanted to comfort her and tell her she was going to be all right, but I could only hold a hand that couldn't feel my touch. I stayed right next to her until the ambulance arrived, then climbed in to accompany her to the hospital. Not two hours earlier, she had left that same hospital as a doctor, only to return now as a patient. A gravely injured one.

As the gurney rolled down the corridor at a swift pace, Micaela's eyes slowly fluttered open. She tried to turn her head to see the figures trotting alongside–I was one of them–but found movement restricted by a brace immobilizing her head. Lacerations striped her face and I wondered if she would need any plastic surgery later on.

She moaned softly.

"Hang in there, ma'am. We're going to fix you up just fine," an orderly assured her. They steered the gurney into a large examination area divided by curtains into smaller compartments. They slid Micaela into one of them and several nurses went to work, one taking vital signs while another began peeling and cutting away bloodied clothing.

"Oh, my God, it's Dr. Pressman. Iris, get the chief resident down here," the second nurse directed. An aide ran to make the page while the nurse tried to distract Micaela from her pain. "We know you love your work, Dr. Pressman, but didn't you get enough of this place for one day?"

Micaela tried to smile but managed only a grimace. The nurse patted her hand. "It's okay; don't try to talk. The doc will be here in a jiffy to give you something for the pain. We need to call your husband and let him know you're here."

Micaela summoned all her strength and whispered an adamant "No."

The nurse frowned. "You don't want your husband?"

"Saul...Saul McBride...come...right away."

The nurse patted her hand again. I could tell she considered Micaela disoriented if not delirious. "That's right," she soothed. "Once your husband is notified, he'll call anyone you want."

"No!" The ferocity of her reply startled the nurse. "Call 410...36..." The nurse leaned in closer to hear the fading whispers. "Write down...410...366...91. Saul...please. Please!" She grimaced again as the pain intensified.

Not wanting to agitate her any further, the nurse grabbed the clipboard with Micaela's chart and scribbled Saul's name and phone number along the margin. She tore off the corner with the information and handed it to Iris. "Call this person right away and notify him that Dr. Pressman had been in an accident and is asking for him."

Micaela visibly relaxed. "Thank you."

Iris nodded and started for the desk phone. The nurse stopped her with a hand on her arm. "Tell him nothing specific about her condition," she cautioned. "Only that she insisted we call him."

* * *

They stabilized Micaela and transferred her to a private room. She drifted in and out of consciousness, unaware of her surroundings or the staff's ministrations. Saul was horrified to learn of the accident and came at once to the hospital, accompanied by the omnipresent Mary Lynn. I didn't imagine for a second that Mary Lynn had concern for anything other than the possible disruption of her vacation plans. She put on a good show for everyone, exuding compassion for the McBrides' longtime friend, crying on cue and wiping an occasional tear from her waterproof black lashes. The bitch really missed her calling. This was another Oscar-worthy performance.

At Micaela's bedside, Saul looked down at her in deep anguish. He didn't understand why she had been so insistent on seeing him right away, but in her present condition he couldn't very well ask. He queried Gerry Pressman, wondering if he had any idea what prompted Micaela's request. Gerry couldn't think of anything offhand, and was really too upset to care.

The trio maintained a vigil in Mic's room long into the night. At one-thirty in the morning, the nurse came in to chart Micaela's vital signs. She took one look at Gerry and said, "Dr. Pressman, you're ready to drop. Why don't you go lie down for a while in the residents' lounge? You can get some rest and be nearby in case your wife takes a turn for the worse."

Gerry agreed. Bleary-eyed, he shook Saul's hand and thanked him for coming. "Whatever Mic was talking about, we'll just have to wait until she can tell us herself. Why don't you take Mary Lynn on home now? I'm going to get a little shut-eye myself."

Saul glanced at Mary Lynn who tenderly smoothed a few errant hairs from Micaela's moist forehead. "If you don't mind, we'd like to stay just a little while longer."

Gerry gave him a grateful look. "Of course. And Saul, that's one special lady you've got in your life now. I know Judith would be happy for you." He caught Mary Lynn's eye across the room and lifted his chin at her in goodbye before he quit the room.

Sometimes life is like a bad soap opera. Not ten minutes after Gerry left to get some sleep, Micaela stirred and moaned. Saul sprang from the faux leather wing chair in the corner, and Mary Lynn straightened against the wall where she leaned. Micaela's eyes opened to slits once, twice, then closed again. Saul took her hand where it rested on a sheet yellowed from repeated bleachings. At his touch, she opened her eyes again and kept them open.

Relief flooded Saul's features. I don't think any of us realized how frightened he was over Micaela's situation. Or was it guilty contrition? He'd all but ignored her ever since Mary Lynn took over his social life. If Micaela didn't make it, he would have to live with that. The prospect must have shamed him.

Micaela gazed at him. "Saul," she whispered.

"Hey, beauty, welcome back. You really gave us a scare."

"Must tell you...something..." Micaela struggled to get the words out, her brain foggy from medication. "Jude said...don't go."

Saul exchanged glances across the bed with Mary Lynn. *Jude said?*

"She must have been dreaming," Mary Lynn proffered.

"Yes...dream," Micaela croaked. "About Jude...warn you...not to go."

"Not go where, Micaela?" Mary Lynn asked, ever so sweet.

"Zea...New Zea...danger..."

Saul gently replaced Micaela's hand on the bed. He looked at Mary Lynn and inclined his head toward the door.

When they were out of Micaela's earshot he said low, "I think she's trying to say she had a dream that something bad happened in New Zealand. I think I know why. Maybe she feels protective of her best friend's husband, so she dreams of Judith and our trip." His expression turned thoughtful. "It is odd, though."

"What?"

"Have you forgotten already? Only a few nights ago I had a similar dream."

"Now, Saul, don't start reading too much into coincidence. You just said it's not surprising that Micaela dreamed about Judith. It's not unusual for you to dream about her, either."

From the bed, Micaela called his name, a note of urgency in her weak voice. Saul and Mary Lynn instantly went to her side. She struggled to prop herself up on her elbows.

"Micaela, don't," Mary Lynn implored. "Saul, you better get Gerry. She seems overwrought."

The residents' lounge was three floors below. Mary Lynn watched surreptitiously from the doorway until she saw the elevator doors close with Saul inside. She pushed the heavy door to Micaela's room closed and hurried back to the bed.

"Saul? Where's...get...Saul..." Micaela tried again to push herself into a sitting position.

"No need to get worked up, honey." Mary Lynn pacified with a pseudo-smile. "Saul will be back. I just want to speak to you alone for a minute."

Listening for telltale footsteps in the corridor, she leaned down until her face was only inches away from Micaela's. "Now you listen good. Don't bother trying to talk Saul out of this trip. You'll only wear yourself out. Besides, there's nothing you can do to stop us. Saul has too much sense to pay attention to your silly little dream."

The pseudo-smile vanished, replaced by a menacing Mary Lynn who meant business. "I'm warning you, Micaela. Don't say anything to upset Saul. He's been through enough as it is."

As she straightened, she spotted a bottle of isopropyl alcohol on the bedside commode. She pulled a tissue from the box, wadded it into a ball, and soaked it thoroughly with the alcohol. She took care to secure the cap and replace the bottle in the same position she had found it. In one swift, calculated movement, she pressed the sodden tissue firmly against a deep gash above Micaela's right eyebrow. Micaela stiffened and her back arched, but she couldn't summon the strength to call for help.

Mary Lynn relocated the tissue to a reddened laceration under Micaela's chin. "Get the message?" She moved her hand back to Mic's forehead and squeezed the tissue until alcohol droplets fell into the wound. Micaela moaned and squirmed.

My hands balled into fists and I clenched my teeth, longing to wring Mary Lynn's ivory neck. I had to witness this act of deliberate cruelty, yet I could do nothing about it. If only I knew how to move objects, I'd take that glass bud vase Saul bought downstairs in the gift shop and smash it over her carefully coiffed head.

Mary Lynn stuffed the damp, pink-stained tissue into her purse, her timing impeccable. The door swung open and Saul walked in with a weary and worried Gerry.

"What's going on? Is she okay?"

"She seems a little agitated," Mary Lynn told him, the epitome of compassion and sympathy. I'll say this much for her, she was the consummate pro at switching personae.

Gerry leaned over his wife and held her hand. Mary Lynn whispered to Saul, "Let's go. I think we've been too much for her."

Saul was reluctant to leave, but Mary Lynn appeared so concerned for Micaela's condition that he conceded. "I'll come back tomorrow, Mic, Gerry," he promised.

A shiver ran the length of my spine. I was truly frightened, not just for Micaela but for Saul. Until now I hadn't realized the depths of Mary Lynn's true nature. If she could maliciously torture a bedridden, injured woman, what could she do to my husband?

Indeed, what couldn't she do?

Chapter Fifteen

As it turned out, Saul did not return to the hospital the next day, or the day after that. He checked often with Gerry Pressman on Micaela's condition—which remained critical—but Mary Lynn managed to keep him so busy with pre-departure errands that he never seemed to find time to go see Micaela for himself. A couple of times I saw him arrive home laden with packages. Mary Lynn insisted they buy just the right hiking boots and polar fleece jackets. And a new video camera. She planned to capture the whole thing for posterity when Saul made his momentous bungee jump in Queenstown.

When I wasn't monitoring Saul's situation, I kept my own vigil at Micaela's bedside. She hadn't improved, but she wasn't getting any worse, either. The only visitors allowed to see her were Gerry and her parents, so it remained quiet in her hospital room. Which is why it startled me to feel a touch on my shoulder as I sat in the corner chair.

I squealed in surprise, glad the commotion wouldn't disturb Micaela. "What are you doing here?"

"You are difficult to locate these days, Judith," Ashraf replied. "This is the only place where I could be certain to find you. I must speak with you for a moment."

He led the way to the door, gesturing me to follow. I didn't know why he had to leave the room to talk to me. We could have sat in the middle of Micaela's bed while we talked and no one would be the wiser. Nevertheless, I followed him into the hallway. Along the way, he glided very close to Micaela's father. Arthur Hurwitz put a hand to the back of his head as if something had brushed against him. He glanced over his shoulder, then shrugged.

"What is it, Arthur?" Beverly Hurwitz asked.

"Nothing. Just a fly or something."

Ashraf paused outside Micaela's door. "My sincerest condolences on your friend's condition, Judith. Is she at all improved?"

I shook my head. "No, and I'm getting really worried about her. Between the accident and Saul's predicament, my mind is swimming." I pressed my fingers to my temples.

Ash weighed his words. "Yes. I know you have a great deal on your mind." He cleared his throat and his tone became stern. "But I must speak to you about your obligations. You have been neglecting your duties at the Animal Compound."

"Siobhan agreed to cover for me. Besides, I happen to think I have a greater responsibility right now to Saul and Micaela."

"I will not try again to persuade you that these responsibilities you feel to your husband and friend are misguided, albeit well-intentioned. I am here only to remind you of the obligations you have on level Seven."

"You picked a fine time to lecture me."

"My dear, Judith, I am not here because I desire it. I bring you this message at the behest of the Spirit Council."

"What have they got to say about it?"

He gave me a long look. "They have a great deal to say about it. I am merely their messenger. Perhaps you should give the matter some thought."

A moan came from Micaela's room and Ash glanced past me toward the sound. "You may return to your friend now. But please, do not forget your other friends. They need you, too."

Then he disappeared.

I was at a loss as to why the Spirit Council would consider a few missed shifts at the Jungle more important than my husband and my best friend. It's not as though I hadn't arranged for someone to cover for me. I thought that, under the circumstances, I'd been damned responsible.

I threw my hands up and went back into Mic's room. I'd mend fences with the Council when all this was over. Right now, Micaela needed me.

Two days before Saul and Mary Lynn planned to leave for New Zealand, I happened to be at the house with Saul when he telephoned Micaela's hospital room. Gerry had stepped out with his father-in-law for some coffee, so Beverly Hurwitz answered the phone and told Saul that

Micaela's status had been upgraded from critical to serious. She was stable, a good sign, but she was by no means out of the woods yet.

Saul thanked her and hung up. He walked into the bedroom where Mary Lynn sorted clothes for the trip.

She glanced at him as she discarded a pair of shoes from the to-pack pile. "How is she?"

"She's been upgraded from critical to serious. But at least she's stable."

"That's good news. She must be getting better or they wouldn't have upgraded her."

"Yeah, well, serious is serious." Saul put his hands in his pockets and toyed with loose change. "Mary Lynn, I've been thinking. Maybe we should postpone the trip."

Mary Lynn dropped the sweater she was folding and put her hands on her hips. "We're leaving in two days, Saul. Why are you starting this now?"

"I can't go halfway around the world with Micaela in this condition. Not in good conscience."

By now I was familiar with the telltale signs that Mary Lynn was fighting to remain calm when she really wanted to explode with rage. Her body went rigid, her teeth clenched, and a tiny muscle in her cheek started moving back and forth. She got riled so often these days that I quickly came to recognize the signals.

"I understand how you feel, Saul, but we aren't leaving her alone. Her own husband and her parents are with her."

"That's not the point. Don't you think going on

vacation now looks rather shallow, as if we're indifferent to the situation? For Pete's sake, Micaela was Judith's best friend."

The muscle in Mary Lynn's cheek started to work faster as she gnashed her teeth together. I was surprised steam didn't come out of her ears. "Micaela is your friend too, which is why I'm sure she would not want to be responsible for canceling your vacation plans."

Saul grew thoughtful. "To be honest, I don't think she was all that keen on the idea. She kept trying to tell us not to go, that something about it was dangerous."

"That was the morphine talking. And of course she would think it's dangerous. Friends don't like friends jumping off cliffs."

Such a witty *bon mot*!

One side of Saul's mouth went up and Mary Lynn relaxed, back in command. She took his face in her hands and kissed him playfully. "Now come on and get packing. I can't do all of it myself." She resumed folding a stack of Saul's cargo shorts.

Saul caught her arm and turned her to face him. "I'm sorry, M.L. I just don't think I should go, not with Micaela so ill. I'm sorry." His gaze held hers for a long moment. Mary Lynn's eyes sparked fire and she jerked her arm away. Saul reasoned that he'd best wait out the storm and retreated from the bedroom before Mary Lynn started one of her tirades.

Her furious eyes bored into his back. Nobody walked

away from Mary Lynn. "Saul! You come back here!"

He didn't.

She smacked a fist into her open hand and uttered an impotent growl. She grabbed a hairbrush lying among the clothes strewn on the bed and hurled it at Saul's departing head. Too late, it hit the closing door with a loud *thwack*.

I stood with my mouth open, as surprised as Mary Lynn. I don't know how he did it, but my husband finally managed to stand up to her. It would have been nice if he had developed this gumption earlier–maybe my picture wouldn't still be in the dresser drawer. Better late than never, though.

I should have been jumping for joy over this unexpected turn of events, but for some reason the victory wasn't as sweet as I'd imagined. Perhaps what happened next eclipsed it.

Hissy fit over, Mary Lynn composed herself and went out to the kitchen to talk to Saul. He was perched on a stool at the counter, reading the paper.

She approached him, careful to keep her tone conciliatory. "Saul, I'd like to talk to you."

The newspaper lowered, revealing an impassive face. "There's nothing more to talk about, M.L. I mean it this time. I've decided to stay and that's that."

"I know, darling, and I respect your decision. I was wrong to react that way. I just wanted to know if you would mind very much if I went without you."

His eyebrows went up. "You still want to go? By

yourself?"

"Well, if you'd rather I didn't..."

"Hell no, I think it's a great idea! To tell you truth, I was feeling a little guilty about making you miss the trip you'd looked forward to for so long. This way, neither of us has to feel guilty."

This couldn't have been the response Mary Lynn hoped for. She had something up her sleeve. All I could do was wait and see what it was.

"Okay, it's settled, then," she said. "Will you at least see me off at the airport?"

"Of course I will. I can drop you on my way to the hospital."

The hands by her side clenched into fists again, but I was the only one to notice. Without another word, she turned on her heel and went to finish packing.

I wasn't convinced for one minute that she would go because she didn't want to miss the bungee jump of a lifetime. There had to be more to it. With Mary Lynn, there always was.

I was bent on finding out, even if it meant following her on her solo trip to New Zealand. First, I decided to heed Ashraf's advice. It couldn't hurt to tie up any loose ends on Seven so I could leave with a clear conscience.

I spent the next two days working in the Jungle and catching up with Siobhan and Suse J, careful to avoid the subject of where I'd been spending my time of late. It wasn't easy. I had to keep up a steady stream of chatter to stave off the questions I knew would come spilling out if I allowed them to get a word in edgewise. I didn't know if it was due to my flapping tongue or their own diplomacy, but either way, they never said a word about it.

I admit it was good to see everyone up There. Tension flowed out of me the minute I came back. In my preoccupation with everything happening on earth, I didn't realize how much I missed my celestial life: the little pleasantries, my job at the Jungle, the carefree existence. Yet no matter what I did, my thoughts always stayed with Micaela and Saul. I should have experienced nothing but peace up There, but anxiety to discover Mary Lynn's real agenda increasingly distracted me. Time to wrap things up on Seven and get back to the real problem.

Siobhan hid her disapproval and assured me she had no trouble continuing to fill in for me at the Jungle. Suse J, on the other hand, was less than enthusiastic. When I told her about my intention to follow Mary Lynn to New Zealand, she didn't try to talk me out of it, but the resignation in her voice betrayed her true feelings.

"I guess you gotta do what you gotta do," she sighed.

"Why does everyone act as though I'm committing a crime or something?"

"Of course you're not committing a crime, Jude. It's the 'something' I'm worried about."

She may not have put up the supportive front Siobhan did, but at least she had the good grace not to lecture me. I knew well everyone's opinions about my endeavor, but I didn't want to hear it just then. Plenty of time for that when I returned, once I had satisfied myself that Saul was safe.

The respite on Seven was just the break I needed from the enervating task of keeping myself in the astral plane near earth. I hadn't realized how spent I had become. So with renewed energy and a sense of obligation fulfilled, I followed the passengers up the Jetway to board the Qantas 747 that would take us to Auckland.

The final boarding call was announced, but still no sign of Mary Lynn. I hung out by the forward galley of the plane to wait. She was probably in the ladies' room in the terminal. Sure enough, only a minute or two later she came through the forward entry and returned the flight attendants' greetings. She gave a lingering smile to the pilot standing in the cockpit doorway with a Styrofoam coffee cup in his hand. His eyes followed her as she slid past the first-row passengers trying to stuff their belongings into the already-full overhead bins.

She stopped at the third row of seats and set her carry-on bag in the aisle seat. First class. I might have known. She must have turned in Saul's coach ticket to upgrade her own.

Someone already sat next to the window in that row, a wide-open newspaper acting as a barricade against whomever sat alongside. I helped myself to the vacant seat directly across the aisle. The Blonde Bombshell half-turned toward the window, already deep in conversation with her seatmate who had abandoned his newspaper.

A pleasant male voice responded to Mary Lynn's pleasantries. Gee, why wasn't I surprised? She didn't waste time or money–Saul's money, that is. He paid for this trip, and here she already made a new, er...'friend.' She fluffed out her peroxide mane as the gate crew secured the forward door and the flight attendants began their litany of safety instructions.

Four empty Smirnoff Silver miniatures were lined up on the tray table in front of Mary Lynn and her...companion. A thin blue airline blanket had been draped over their laps and hung to the floor. With a girlish giggle, she slipped a hand underneath.

Not six hours away from Saul and she picks up a stranger on a plane. So much for fidelity. I hoped she didn't come home and give Saul a disease.

The curtain separating first class from coach parted and a flight attendant came up the aisle toward the galley.

"Someone's coming," Mary Lynn whispered as she withdrew her hand.

"I was just about to," the male voice breathed.

Mary Lynn flushed with the perverse pleasure of almost being caught. She reclined her seat all the way back, affording me a clear view of her latest conquest.

It was Saul.

I didn't think I could possibly have been more shocked than when Saul backed out of the trip two days ago. I was wrong. His no-nonsense declaration then had made me secure in the knowledge that his bungee jumping days were over before they started. Mary Lynn strikes again. How did she manage to change Saul's mind when he'd been so adamant? More to the point, how could I save his life now that it was too late to stop him from going?

At least I had one consolation. Saul's change-of-change-of-heart could only mean that Micaela's condition had improved. I had that to be thankful for. As for what lay ahead, I had not a clue. I knew only that I had my work cut out for me.

Chapter Sixteen

Seeing Saul on his way to New Zealand really shook me up. I couldn't think straight while sitting across the aisle from the newest members of the Mile High Club. So I retreated to Seven for a few days to regroup. I went about my everyday routine in a daze, unsure how to proceed and wondering if my efforts had been all for naught, anyway. Mary Lynn was like herpes: impossible to get rid of and frequently painful.

I sat alone on a garden bench outside the Social Hall when Ashraf came walking toward me, his slim body erect and dignified, as always. I had a pretty good idea what he had come to talk to me about it, but I beat him to the punch.

"I haven't visited Saul in days. See? I'm being good." I didn't add that my only reason for staying away was that I hadn't set a new course of action.

Oddly enough, Ash didn't respond. He just looked down at me in his gentle way. Had what I said even registered?

"I'm afraid I have some bad news for you, Judith."

My smile faded. "It's Saul, isn't it? Has he–"

Ash shook his head. "But I am afraid it is someone also very dear to you." He gave me a moment to think.

I frowned and cocked my head at him.

"Micaela has passed on."

He was mistaken, of course. "No, no. Micaela is getting better," I insisted. "Otherwise Saul wouldn't have changed his mind again and left for New Zealand."

"No, my dear. Her condition worsened yesterday. She lapsed into a coma and then experienced complete renal failure. I'm afraid Micaela's earthly life is at an end."

And I hadn't been there...

"What about machines?" My voice came out as a croak. "They can take over for failing kidneys. Surely she's on machines?"

"Her husband had her removed from life support equipment. He said her wishes were not to cling to a body kept alive by artificial means."

I struggled to process this stunning news. This wasn't supposed to happen. Not to Micaela. Not this way.

Ash sat down beside me on the garden bench. "Micaela is waiting for you at the Welcome Center, Judith. Go to her. I am certain you two have a great deal to say to each other."

I nodded dumbly. There were so many things I had to say to her: that this wasn't what I intended when I visited her in dreams; that I was blinded by my cavalier faith in her friendship and in my love for Saul...

"Come, Judith. Go and greet your friend," Ashraf urged. "She is waiting for you." He stood up to face me and held out his hand as if asking me to dance.

I put my hand in his and let him lead me away.

Stunned, I seemed to move in slow motion, paralyzed by this illogical development, and more than a little rueful. How much of it was my fault?

As soon as I walked into the Welcome Center with Ash, memories of my last time there came flooding back. I had been the guest of honor then, awestruck by the surroundings and lighthearted about the future. The place was just as beautiful now, but my heart was far from light. I was the one responsible for Micaela's arrival up Here before her time.

I tried to put on a happy face to greet my friend, but I just couldn't manage it. No matter how delighted I was to have her with me again, there was no getting around that her death had been caused by my own hubris. Gooseflesh rose on my arms. What if Mic was angry with me? She had every right to be, but I prayed she wasn't. I could endure anything but her displeasure.

She perched on a low stone wall, swinging her legs and idly kicking it with her heels. Emotion rushed through my head like whitewater rapids, pushing aside the guilt as easily as if it was a piece of driftwood. My Micaela.

She caught sight of me then and her legs stopped swinging. She leaped off the wall; I broke into a run and we collided into each other's arms. It wasn't all that long ago that our spirits had visited while she slept, but this reunion was different. Both unencumbered by physical bodies now, we were free to reinforce the close connection of our souls. It occurred to me that we must have shared this moment before, in other lifetimes. Ours was a friendship that spanned incarnations.

We let go just enough to stand and look at each other. To my relief, she didn't seem angry, though I couldn't have blamed her if she had been. In my fixation to save my husband, I had cut her life short. I wanted to take it all back, but it was too late.

We embraced again and I never wanted to get go. "Mic, I'm so sorry," I whispered into her fresh-smelling hair.

She pulled back and looked at me. "I thought you'd be glad that I'm here."

"I'm glad our spirits are together again, of course, but Micaela, I'm to blame for your accident and death. It wasn't your time, and if I hadn't asked you to help me warn Saul..."

She cocked her head. "How do you know it wasn't my time?"

"Because if you weren't on your way to see Saul, you wouldn't have been in that accident."

"Judith McBride, you haven't learned much up Here, have you? Do you honestly believe you are so omnipotent as to cause my death?"

I blinked, caught off guard. I was prepared for anger, but she was mad for the wrong reason. "I–I didn't mean it like that. I only meant that by involving you in my problem, I contributed to your death."

"That's nothing but an ego trip."

Oh, Micaela. Don't spoil it...

I hung my head like a chastened child and she softened.

"Jude, I don't mean to hurt your feelings, but think about it. Nobody's death is untimely, even though it might seem that way. You should know that better than I. Why, every soul knows the ultimate outcome of an earthly life before she accepts it. I went into this incarnation with my eyes and heart wide open. I was destined to die at this time in this life."

What she said was true, but harder to accept when the situation was personal.

"There's something else... Maybe it will make things a bit clearer." Micaela swallowed. "For a while now, I've had certain...feelings for Saul."

"For Saul? *My* Saul?"

She nodded.

"What about Gerry?"

"I love Gerry, of course, but it has nothing to do with what I feel for Saul." She peered at me for a reaction. "I never acted on it, Jude. I want you to know that. Saul never knew; at least, not that he let on. Neither did Gerry."

As well as I knew my friend, I had never suspected this. Other than numbness, I felt devoid of emotion. But my best friend just told me she had the hots for my husband. Shouldn't I feel *something*?

"Why are you telling me this, Micaela?"

"To prove to you that you weren't responsible for my death. Why do you think I was in such a hurry to see Saul?"

I didn't hesitate. "Because you're my friend and you wanted to help me, to help both of us."

"Of course I'm your friend, Jude, and of course I wanted to help you. But don't you see? If my own feelings for Saul weren't so distorted, I might not have acted so rashly. That's really what caused the accident. I let my emotions override my better judgment. My mind that night was definitely not on driving." Her expression went from stern to meek. "Do you hate me?"

Cold numbness melted into a warm tide of feeling. "I could never hate you, Micaela. Even if you and Saul had had a torrid affair, I wouldn't be much of an evolved soul not to forgive you. But hey, it never happened, so there's nothing to forgive." I gave her a rueful smile. "I almost wish it had happened. If you and Saul had hooked up, he might not have fallen under Mary Lynn's spell. Then none of this would be happening. You wouldn't have had a fatal car accident and Saul wouldn't be enroute to a death trap in New Zealand."

Poor Gerry Pressman had been left out of the equation altogether.

A soft-spoken voice made us both turn. "It's time for your orientation, Micaela." An elegant young woman stood behind us, her hands clasped in front of her.

"Oh, Judith, I want you to meet Eleanor, my spirit guide." Micaela's manner with this stranger was free and easy.

Eleanor bobbed a polite curtsey and studied me with quiet interest. I nodded to her, taking in the elaborate hairdo and the empire-style gown. She looked liked she'd stepped out of a Jane Austen novel.

"I am very pleased to make your acquaintance, Judith. Micaela has told me much of you."

Funny, she mentioned nothing to me about you... "Thank you."

She turned to her charge. "I do apologize for the interruption, but you must come now to orientation. Judith, we must beg your leave to excuse us."

"Do you have to go right now?" We had so much more to talk about. I turned to Eleanor. "Can't she come along in a little bit?"

Mic squeezed my hand. "I have to go. But I'll see you again soon. Please don't worry, Jude. Everything will turn out for the good."

"Really?" I sounded like an eager seven-year-old in need of reassurance, but maybe she knew something I didn't. Did she hint that Saul would be all right, but couldn't leak any details in front of Eleanor? Maybe we had gotten through to Saul after all, and he decided not to do the bungee jump. The possibility made my heart pound.

Micaela squeezed my hand again, bringing me back from my racing thoughts. A peck on the cheek, and she and Eleanor disappeared into the mist.

"Hey, wait," I called after them. "What level will you be on?" Too late. They didn't hear me. But I didn't really need to be told what I already knew. Micaela couldn't be assigned anywhere but to level Seven with me. I had confidence in her spiritual evolution.

Who says I can't change destiny?

With Micaela busy with in-processing, I took advantage of the time to see what was happening with Saul. He was in Queenstown by now, but I didn't know when they were scheduled to go to Skipper's Canyon Bridge. That was one excursion I didn't want to miss. My certainty of his demise on this trip hadn't wavered, and I wasn't about to give up now and stand idle while my husband got himself killed. No matter how many times I'd been reminded not to interfere, I just couldn't understand the kind of celestial reasoning that dictated letting the chips fall where they may.

When I caught up with Saul and Mary Lynn in their hotel, they were just getting out of bed, despite the fact that it was three in the afternoon in New Zealand. Whether from jet lag or something else that had kept them there so late, I didn't really want to know.

They spent the remainder of the afternoon in the room, going through the tour brochures piled on the table. Seven o'clock rolled around, and I followed them to dinner at the hotel restaurant. Mary Lynn hadn't wanted to eat there. She wanted to explore and find a place with 'local color,' but Saul hadn't felt up to it after the long trip from the States. On this rare occasion, she acquiesced without so much as a pout. In fact, she purred her agreement. "The sooner we have dinner, the sooner we can go back to bed."

And I thought they were so worn out from the journey.

I gave Mary Lynn an ethereal glare. *I hope the long*

flight made you retain water. The Curse of Judith. *May you be as spiny as a puffer fish and just as bloated.*

Saul didn't take the suggestive bait like he usually did. He had something else on his mind. "I just don't know about tomorrow, M.L. This time we might be going too far."

He was still having second thoughts about the bungee jump. Good. Great!

Mary Lynn's eyes welled with tears. Saul reached for her hand, but she snatched it away.

"I know this disappoints you, M.L., but one of us has to be practical," he consoled. "You could get yourself killed."

Ever the drama queen, she dabbed the linen napkin at the corners of her exotically lined eyes. What did Mary Lynn Bernhardt have planned for Act Two?

"Saul, darling, we've come all this way," she said in a tiny voice that held just the right hint of helpless deference without sounding whiny. "Now you're going to tell me you won't go through with it? I can't believe you'd be so selfish."

The dark circles of fatigue under Saul's eyes became even darker as he faced another battle with Mary Lynn's obstinate nature. She sat silent, looking hurt and dejected. Two fat teardrops obligingly rolled down her puffy cheeks (she *had* retained water) and I gave the performance an appreciative round of otherworldly applause.

Saul gave a resigned sigh. It was pathetic how easily he gave in to Mary Lynn's transparent theatrics. What had happened to the self-possessed man I had married? For that matter, what had happened to the confident man of a few days ago who insisted he should not go on vacation just now? Gee, I wish had known he was this malleable during our marriage. I would have held out more often for what *I* wanted.

It was nonetheless difficult to see the pile of mush that once been my Saul. I shook my head to clear away thoughts of his complete one-eighty and bring myself back to the problem at hand. I wasn't there to cast aspersions; I had a mission. In fact, I could see more clearly than ever that Saul needed me, and I wasn't about to let him down.

Chapter Seventeen

I waited until after breakfast the next day before showing up at Saul and Mary Lynn's room, hoping my timing would be on target to hitch a ride with them to the bungee jump site. I was no longer pissed off or even surprised that Saul had once again allowed himself to be manipulated. I merely accepted it and went ahead with my plans as though his earlier decision to forego this entire trip—much less yesterday's second thoughts—had never been made.

From their conversations during the trip's planning stages, I knew that we were all heading for a location near the picturesque mountain resort of Queenstown on New Zealand's South Island. The drive up the mountain road to the bungee site was reputed to be as treacherous as the other parts of the excursion, and I intended to be in the car with them.

When I got to their room, they were dressed and ready to leave. The vestiges of an elaborate room service breakfast lay on the table by the window. An empty champagne bottle rested in the watery remains of ice cubes in a bucket, next to a carton of orange juice.

Room service. Complete with mimosas. I used to think

it was a special treat when Saul and I ordered from the hang-over-the-doorknob continental breakfast menu.

I trailed after Mary Lynn and Saul to the hotel lot where they had parked their rented Audi, climbed into the back seat, and waited. Saul fumbled with the keys, then unlocked the passenger door for Mary Lynn. The chivalrous gesture made me smile. Shades of the old Saul, the often clumsy, gentle person I had partnered myself with for that particular lifetime. If only it hadn't been such a brief one.

Mary Lynn stepped on the running board of the open door and reached inside for the sunglasses resting on the dashboard. She put them on and slammed the car door shut. The pair walked back toward the hotel lobby entrance.

Now what?

I scrambled out of the car and hurried to catch up.

"–why they don't allow rental cars on that road," Mary Lynn was saying.

"What's the difference, as long as the tour company is picking us up?"

"It just seems silly to have our own wheels and not be able to use them. I prefer traveling under my own steam."

Saul's voice held the faintest tinge of impatience. "You saw the rental contract, M.L. 'Rental cars are not permitted on the road to Skipper's Canyon Bridge.'"

Before Mary Lynn could continue airing her latest grievance, a van pulled into the hotel's circular drive. The miniature billboard on its roof read *Queenstown Tours* and a painted slogan on the side of the vehicle advertised their specialty: *Take the plungy with Queenstown Bungy.*

I guess the way they spell "death" down Under is B-U-N-G-Y.

An impossibly cheerful blond beach god hopped down from the driver's seat.

"G'day, folks. My name is Trevor and I'll be taking you up to Skipper's Canyon Bridge this morning."

Everyone exchanged greetings, then Saul handed Mary Lynn into the back seat of the van. I climbed in the front seat next to Trevor, noticing the fine blond hairs gleaming against his deeply tanned arms.

"This your first time in New Zealand?" Trevor called over his shoulder as we pulled out of the driveway.

"Yes, it is," Mary Lynn answered. "And we're really looking forward to today."

"Bungy jumped before, have you?"

Saul opened his mouth to reply but before he could say anything, Mary Lynn dug the heel of her hiking boot into his toes. "Once or twice," she said over Saul's yip of protest. "But nothing like Queenstown."

"Too right," Trevor chirped. "People come from all over the world to jump this site. The Queen's granddaughter Zara Phillips made the jump a few years back."

He steered the van into the driveway of another hotel and killed the motor. "Got to pick up another group here, mates. Won't take but a minute." He stepped down from the van and went into the hotel lobby, leaving the three of us alone.

As soon as he walked out of sight, Saul turned to Mary Lynn, furious.

"What the hell was that for?" he demanded, rubbing his foot.

Mary Lynn slid closer to him and ran her hand along his thigh.

I rolled my eyes. Was this the only way she knew to placate him? The woman really needed to broaden her horizons.

"Darling, we don't want anyone to know we've never bungee jumped before," she cooed.

For once, Saul was unmoved. "Why not? We don't have anything to prove."

"I just don't want Trevor patronizing us like we're just another pair of dorky tourists."

Saul wasn't buying. "You're always so worried about what other people think. Why don't you just relax and be yourself? The hell with what other people think."

All right, Saul!

Mary Lynn dropped her hand from his thigh. "You mean the way Judith was. Isn't that what you're saying? That you wish I were more like her?"

"No, M.L., you're missing the point."

"Do you think you would ever have this kind of fun if you were still with Judith? Do you think you would have seen the world or experienced life as I've shown you it can be?"

Saul's eyes narrowed. "That's unfair."

"You bet it's unfair. Unfair to me! I'm tired of forever being compared to *her*." Mary Lynn yanked the door handle open and all but fell out of the van, coming face to face with Trevor and a startled group of four British college kids. She hastened to regain her composure. "Trevor, uh, I just need to pop into the ladies' room. I'll be right back."

She bustled into the hotel, leaving an embarrassed Saul shifting in his seat. The college group snickered among themselves, probably chalking up the Yanks' spat to anxiety about the jump to come.

Still amazed at the unexpected face-off between Saul and Mary Lynn, this was the first time I'd heard him get really angry with her, without regard for the possible repercussions. It seemed there might be hope for him. She hadn't yet whipped him into complete submission.

With the addition of the newcomers, the van got a little cozy. When Mary Lynn returned from the rest room, I moved over in the front seat to make room for her. Not that anyone knew, or that I even really needed to move, but it gave me a reason to sit closer to Trevor of the golden skin and sun-bleached hair. I hadn't been out of circulation so long that I didn't appreciate a fine male specimen when I saw one.

Mary Lynn asked one of the British kids to switch seats with her so she could sit with Saul. I didn't relish the idea of sitting beside Mary Lynn, anyway.

Leaving behind the civilized world of hotels and restaurants, the van tooled through a desolate stretch of savannah. Trevor chattered through the ride, relating bits and pieces of information about Skipper's Canyon Bridge and the Shotover River it spanned. "The drop is sixty-nine meters to the river. It's the highest bungee site you'll find anywhere."

"How much is that in feet?" Saul questioned.

"That's two hundred forty feet to you Yanks."

"That doesn't seem so terribly high," Mary Lynn ventured.

The two English girls in the rearmost seat gave each other a knowing glance. The Yank was definitely a cherry.

"No? Consider that the bungee jumps you see at carnivals and fairs back in the States are typically sixty feet high," Trevor pointed out.

I didn't have to turn around to see Mary Lynn gulp–I heard it.

Trevor turned the van onto a narrow road that didn't look like it led anywhere you'd want to go. When I say narrow, I mean *narrow*. The fact that we drove on the left-hand side, closest to the mountain, made no difference on a road that climbed steeper by the minute. The road's outer edge had no guardrails to keep us from hurtling over.

Inside the van, it grew very quiet.

Saul cleared his throat and tried to break the tension. "Trevor, why is it that rental cars are not allowed on this road?"

"Glad you asked that, mate." Trevor slowed to a stop and pulled up the parking brake handle. He twisted around in his seat and addressed one of the English girls. "Louise, be a love and slide open that door for me."

Louise grasped the handle and pulled open the van door to expose a breathtaking vista. High ridges towered into the sky, the sun sparkling off the mineral deposits embedded in the rock and making lights bounce and spin off the surface. A smattering of dusty scrub was the only real plant life.

Louise reached into her backpack and pulled out a sweatshirt to tug over her head. I realized that the air must be considerably cooler at this altitude, though personally I couldn't tell. It was late summer in this part of the world, but the higher peaks glittered with hoar frost. The whole panorama looked like something from a fairyland.

"Look down," Trevor said.

I leaned toward the open passenger-side window and saw how close we were to the edge. The crumbly lip of the dirt road was a mere two feet from the van. The Brit seated next to me shrieked and clambered over to Trevor's side, flattening me like a grilled-cheese sandwich. Trevor grinned, enjoying the reaction of the girl on his lap. He urged us all to look down the sheer drop of several hundred feet to the bottom of the gorge.

I unwedged myself from the confines of my seatmates to get a good look. The rusted remnants of several vehicles lay in pieces on the craggy rocks at the bottom. Chunks of chrome reflected sunbeams like a signal flare. How I wished Saul would heed their warning.

Trevor nodded toward the wreckage. "That answer

your question, mate?" he asked Saul. "Most people who drive this road are pretty familiar with it, but there are always a few blokes who think they can cheat death. Or sometimes the Yanks forget that we drive on the left. They see a car coming the opposite way, bearing down on them full speed ahead, and they panic. Veer off to the right instead of to the left, and over they go. Happened enough times that the insurance companies won't cover rentals any more."

The van again grew silent.

"Seen enough?" Trevor asked needlessly. "Okey-dokey, mates, slide that door closed and we'll be on our way. Next stop, Skipper's Canyon Bridge!"

Fear for Saul's life renewed itself. Trevor's cavalier attitude didn't sit well with me. What if he was the next driver to go over the cliff?

Two more nerve-wracking miles crept by without incident before we saw a tour mini-bus careening around a bend in the mountain road. It outsized our van by a half and had to be going at least fifty miles an hour.

"Oh, my God," Saul blurted.

I watched in terror as the bus headed right for us. I glanced at Trevor, who appeared unruffled by the scenario. From the way he was smiling, you'd think he planned this as a publicity stunt. He wasn't the least concerned with avoiding the oncoming bus. I clutched the edge of my seat with both hands, unwilling to watch what was coming but unable to tear my eyes away. Even the English girls squealed for Trevor to stop the van. The boys worked hard at staying cool, but their ashen faces told a different story.

Trevor pretended not to hear the girls and began whistling the Beatles' *Drive My Car*. We might just as well have been out for a leisurely Sunday ride.

This was what I'd been so afraid of. I didn't want Saul–or anybody–to die like this. If only I could pluck him out of the van and whisk him back with me to level Seven.

My fingers tightened on the edge of the plastic seat as I braced myself for the inevitable. It would all be over soon.

At the last possible second, Trevor swerved the van hard to the left, causing it to incline up the mountainside and giving the oncoming bus the necessary berth to pass by.

"WHOOEY," Trevor yelled. "How'd you like that, mates?"

"Trevor, you shit, you scared us half to death," Louise shouted from the back. "I've got a mind to report you."

"Come on now, Louise love, you've ridden with me before and know what to expect. I couldn't cheat the others out of the requisite excitement or they'd want their money back."

I turned around to see how Saul fared. Obviously shaken, his face gone white, he appeared to be all right.

Mary Lynn, on the other hand, had fainted dead away.

Chapter Eighteen

Trevor reached into the glove compartment and pulled out a small ampule of spirits of ammonia. He handed it back to Saul who passed it under Mary Lynn's nose. She revived in seconds, trying for all she was worth to maintain her usual aplomb.

She couldn't quite carry it off. She trembled, her face glistened with perspiration, and for once she had nothing to say. What could she say? She had been the one who insisted they embark on this exploit. Her fear and humiliation were self-imposed.

"She all right, mate?" Trevor asked Saul.

He stroked Mary Lynn's hair and gave her a one-armed hug. "She's all right. My lady's a tough cookie."

Yeah. Like hardtack.

Mary Lynn assured Trevor that she was fine and ready to continue, so he started up the motor. The remaining minutes of the ride were quiet, albeit anxious ones, and passed without further incident. When the boat dock finally came into view, sighs of relief went around the van. The name *Last Resort* was painted in jaunty blue letters on the side of the boat tied to the pier. A capable-looking man sat in the captain's seat, not as boyish as Trevor, but just as tanned. I was glad to see he didn't wear the bored look that many locals have when dealing with tourists all season long. He was alert and professional, inspiring confidence. Then again, it might only have been the yachtsman's hat.

Trevor parked on a gravel pad at the road's end, and everyone stepped out of the van, feeling a bit fragile. I heard the rapid thumping in their chests and knew that if I still had a tangible, beating heart it would have been drumming right along with them. That is, if it hadn't arrested altogether by now. But we had made it safely this far, and I checked one item off my list of possible disasters.

While everyone stretched and regrouped after the blood-curdling ride up the mountain, Trevor told us what to expect on the rest of the journey.

"The *Last Resort* will give us all the ride of our lives to Nevis Highwire Station. From there we'll take a gondola halfway across the gorge to the jump station."

"What do you mean by 'the ride of our lives'?" Mary Lynn asked.

Louise stifled a laugh behind her hand. Trevor shot her a warning look.

"You'll see," he promised Mary Lynn.

He unloaded a large duffel bag of equipment from the back of the van and led the parade from the parking pad to the dock, where he introduced the boat captain. "Everybody, this is Ian. He'll be taking care of us today."

Taking care of us. I liked the reassuring sound of that.

Ian nodded and smiled in greeting, pleasant but not the

extrovert Trevor was. Maybe it was just as well. I'm not sure any of us could have handled much more cheek and stress at the same time.

One by one, Trevor handed us into the idling boat. Oily smoke rose from the sputtering motor. He crammed the duffel bag into an empty space by the engine. A wet stain spread across the olive-drab canvas that I fervently hoped was water and not leaking gasoline. I didn't want to add the risk of fire to my worries. After we all found places on the bench seats lining each side, he made sure we were all accounted for. He then reached into a storage compartment in the floor of the cockpit and pulled out an antiquated life vest, the kind with two orange flotation pillows on either side. This one had seen better days. The pillows were smudged with dirt and the ends of the canvas straps frayed.

"Okay, mates, underneath your seat you'll find one of these for each of you. Everyone know how to put them on?"

Mary Lynn and Saul exchanged looks that told me they were as surprised as I that the life jackets weren't the more modern foam vests. They turned them over and around, trying to figure out how they were worn. Only the Brits nodded affirmation to Trevor's rhetorical question, but he didn't seem to notice that.

"Good. Anyone have any trouble, sing out."

Saul helped Mary Lynn slip into her life jacket, the ungainly orange cushions dwarfing her head. She held her arms away from her body as he wound the long canvas straps twice around her waist and clasped them in front. He made sure her vest was secure before he picked up his own.

Saul fumbled with his jacket, the straps all twisted. Mary Lynn made no move to assist him. Too proud to ask for help, he spent a good few minutes trying to free the tangled mess before Trevor noticed and came over to lend a hand.

Shoddy though the life jackets were, I was glad that at least everybody was required to wear them. I tried to look on the bright side and rely on the expertise of Queenstown Tours and in Ian's boating skills. He's probably done this excursion so many times he could do it blindfolded.

Trevor surveyed the assemblage of orange human beanbags. "Everybody all set?" This time nods came from all around. "All right, mateys, hold on!" He nodded to Ian, who threw the throttle full forward.

The boat catapulted into motion with roaring speed. Saul held on to Mary Lynn with one arm and to the rim of the boat with the other. Mary Lynn used both hands to grip the edges of her seat as if her life depended on it, which it probably did.

It soon became evident that Ian's goal was to make us all think that we would crash into the canyon walls. The boat careened through narrow passages in the winding river, cutting corners at the last possible moment. He had perfect mastery of the maneuver, but that didn't stop everyone from screaming each time he did it. Queenstown Tours intended the ride to be as exciting as a roller coaster, and Ian did his best to live up to their reputation. Judging from the terrified expressions on the six ashen faces around me, I think it's safe to say he didn't disappoint.

Despite the boat's lightning speed, the ride seemed endless. I wasn't so far removed from my physical existence that I didn't remember how fear can slow time down to a standstill. I didn't have to fret about my own adrenaline level, but I still worried for Saul, as well as for the others. This seemed a pretty risky way to get some kicks, and certainly not worth dying for.

As our speed began to decrease, I heard surreptitious sighs of relief all around. I think everyone could have used a good, stiff drink. With skill, Ian pulled the boat alongside the small dock at Nevis Highwire Station. Trevor hopped out and secured the boat lines to the cleats attached to the dock. We all stepped out with rubbery legs but the pale faces soon regained healthier hues. Ian helped Trevor unwedge the duffel bag from its storage place and hoist it onto the dock. Then he untied the forward lines and climbed back into the driver's seat. The bow started drifting away from the dock. Trevor freed the stern rope and tossed it inside the boat. "Thanks, mate. See you at the other end."

Ian gave us a salute as he sped away from the dock. The *Last Resort* would return downriver to pick up the bungee jumpers as they completed their jumps.

One more hazard checked off my list, but I couldn't relax yet. Our intrepid band still had the short gondola ride that would take us from the Highwire Station to the actual jump platform on Skipper's Canyon Bridge. This, at least, was familiar transportation. Saul and I had taken a gondola ride one summer in Colorado. In the off-season, when it was cheaper.

We congregated on the platform in front of the gondola and waited for Trevor, who did some last-minute consulting with the lift operator. Unlike the questionable life-saving equipment on the boat, the modern, well-maintained cable car looked dependable enough. So did the conductor in the minuscule, Plexiglas-enclosed cockpit.

Trevor herded us into the open-air gondola. I stepped inside with the others, reminding myself that a snapped cable was just too prosaic and predictable. I couldn't think of any other kind of mishap that could kill everyone. Everything was going to be fine.

The view from the gondola, as intimidating as it was spectacular, drew gasps from even the jaded Brits. The high and irregular canyon walls, Trevor explained, give the bungee jumper a sensation of leaping to the bottom of a deep bucket. The thought made me shiver. This was some people's idea of fun?

I had to admit the cliffs were beautiful compared to the scraggly bluffs we saw from the van driving up the mountain road. In lieu of the dusty scrub, the canyon was dense with ferns and moss, variegated from the random amounts of sunlight reaching them and giving the walls a deceptively velvety façade. A narrow blue-white waterfall bisected the greenery and tumbled to the river far below.

The New Zealand sun sizzled, but high in the open gondola, cool mists kissed our faces, and the combination was delicious.

Halfway across the gorge, the gondola slowed to a stop in front of a covered scaffold enclosed on two sides. On the opposite side of the scaffold, a concrete-and-iron fortified tongue jutted three feet into the abyss. This was the platform from which jumpers took the plunge. A closed gate separated the platform from the main area of the scaffold.

The cable car slipped neatly into a niche, so perfectly flush with the scaffold that disembarking passengers wouldn't have to navigate any gaps. Trevor asked us all to wait until he disembarked first. He heaved the duffel bag onto the scaffold and stepped out of the cable car. He assisted each person off the gondola, gallantly taking the ladies' hands. Just for fun, I availed myself of the courtesy and daintily placed my hand in his as I stepped out. I saw him look at his hand as if he'd never seen it before, then shook it rapidly, as though it had fallen asleep. He flexed and balled it into a fist several times. I couldn't resist a giggle.

All assembled in the enclosure, Trevor secured the car door and gave a thumbs-up to the conductor. The gondola reversed direction to return to the Highwire Station.

Trevor looked at each of us and rubbed his hands together. "All rightey, mates, who's going to be first?"

Louise pressed forward. "I'll have a go."

"Thatta girl, Louise, show 'em how it's done," one her male companions cheered.

"How much do you weigh this time, love?" Trevor asked.

Louise playfully smacked the back of her hand against his chest and made a face. "Same as last year, cheeky. About fifty-two."

Trevor fished in the duffel bag and pulled out a length of bungee cord. Louise plunked herself down on the floor and stretched her legs out full-length in front.

Trevor knelt down to wrap her ankles with terry cloth toweling. "Keeps the bungee straps from cutting into the skin," he explained to us newbies. It hadn't occurred to me that the velocity of the fall and subsequent recoil might cause the bungee harness to cut into the flesh. I bet it hadn't occurred to Saul, either.

Straps firmly fastened around her ankles, Trevor helped Louise to her feet. He swung open the gate to the platform, pushing it all the way back until it abutted the railing, and hooked it into place. My knees went weak as he strode onto the concrete launch pad and attached the heavy clip at the free end of the bungee cord to a thick, doughnut-shaped iron loop on the end of the platform's iron framework. I envied his fearlessness. You couldn't have paid me enough to go near this place during my time on earth.

As for Louise, all she needed was her hands tied behind her back and she would have made the perfect victim in an old pirate movie. It was going to be a short walk on this plank.

Trevor yanked hard on the bungee clip attached to the iron doughnut, double-checking its security. He walked back to Louise and double-checked the straps on the ankle harness. She had the placid, almost indifferent look of a bungee veteran.

"Now, don't be too nervous, love. You know there's always a certain amount of anxiety on the first jump after a long hiatus," Trevor encouraged.

"I'm not nervous," Louise insisted. I guess she wasn't feeling as placid as she looked. Her voice sounded a little tight.

"She's not nervous, she's terrified," one of the boys hooted.

"Is that so, John?" Louise retorted. "I'm not the one making my very first jump today, so I'd zip my lip if I were you."

John's friendly goading renewed her confidence. She bunny-hopped onto the launch pad, supporting herself with both hands on the railings on either side.

"In fact, I think I'll take the first lift out of here." She shuffled to the tongue's very edge.

Trevor gave a long whistle. "She's a brave one, mates."

I wondered what made Louise especially brave, other than the fact that she was about to hurl herself off a very high place.

Trevor took a walkie-talkie from the holder clipped to his belt and spoke to Ian waiting in the boat below with a second crewman. "All right, Louise, off you go."

Louise took a few deep breaths. Inhaling a final time, she gave a bloodcurdling whoop and yelled, "Going down!" She swung her arms and jumped feet first off the platform.

The entire group–including me–leaned over the scaffold's railing to watch her descent. Louise sank like a stone for about twenty meters before the bungee cord slowed her descent. It reached the end of its length and recoiled, flipping her upside down. There was an eerie silence as she skyrocketed aloft in a repeat cycle.

She was on her second time downward before we heard anything from her. She shouted in triumph, flying heavenward again, a little slower this time and not as high.

"Louise just performed what we call 'the elevator,'" Trevor told us as we watched. "That's jumping feet-first. It's pretty hairy; I'm surprised she went that way."

"Hell, John practically dared her to," the other girl remarked, eyeing the culprit. He raised his hands and widened his eyes. *Who, me?*

The bungee cycle repeated twice more before Louise slowed down enough for Ian to grab her and pull her into the boat. The other crewmember unfastened her ankle straps. Ian caught Louise neatly in his arms as she fell loose from her bonds. He set her on her feet, keeping a hold on her until assured of her balance. She took a seat and waved enthusiastically at the five heads peering over the scaffold high above the river. A collective cheer rose from the group.

Ian gunned the engine and *Last Resort* sped off in a blur for the dock where Louise would wait for the others. After everyone had jumped and assembled there, the boat would take us back to the pier where Trevor had parked the van. We watched in awe from the scaffold as it cornered the rocks at high speed and disappeared around the bend, seeing the 'ride of our lives' from a new perspective, even more frightening from this vantage point than when we had been passengers.

The noise of the engine faded in the distance. A murmur spread within the band of brazen adventurers who suddenly didn't seem so brazen. Even John and the other two kids hung back a little.

Trevor looked from one to the other.

"So who's next?"

Chapter Nineteen

"Me!"

Four pairs of eyes turned to the voice that piped up so eagerly.

I had figured Mary Lynn would insist that Saul go before she did, just in case anything went wrong. Plus, she'd be there to make sure he didn't back out at the last minute. Considering the way he'd vacillated about the whole expedition, it seemed a realistic possibility that he could change his mind...again. I expected her to push him off, if necessary.

Mary Lynn stood at the open gate to the launch pad in all her glory and jump gear. She hesitated a minute or two, either gathering courage or building dramatic suspense. Probably both. Trevor stood to one side with his arms folded, letting her take all the time she needed to psych herself up. When she nodded her head, Saul gave her an *adieu* kiss and backed up to the interior of the scaffold.

Trevor bent down to check the ankle straps one more time. "Now don't be a daredevil like Louise," he warned. "She took the hard way down. When you're ready, just let yourself fall head first, like you're diving into a swimming pool. The bungee will do the rest."

Mary Lynn nodded and gave him a thin smile, her Adam's apple lurching upward in a heavy gulp. She moved in choppy little steps to the edge of the platform, not stopping until her toes projected out into nothingness.

Trevor began a countdown. "Five. Four. Three."

The whole group chimed in. "Two. One. Bungy!"

Mary Lynn spread her arms wide and lifted her chin like she was Donna DeVarona. She sprang off the platform in an admittedly graceful swan dive.

I dashed to the railing to watch. Within seconds her balletic pose became one of flailing limbs accompanied by piercing screams.

Suddenly she stopped screaming, as if someone had clamped a hand over her mouth. I tried to hope that she hadn't had a coronary.

The bungee cord stretched to its limit, then raised her almost halfway to the height of the platform as it snapped back in the opposite direction. As she rose nearer to us, I saw a happy glow of accomplishment, restoring the color to her chalky face. She sent out a cheer of victory to everyone above and below.

"Not bad," commented John. I sensed his own apprehension growing.

Trevor turned to Saul. "Ready, mate? Step up, you're next."

This was it. I had to stop him *now*. On impulse I stuck my foot out to trip him as he crossed to the front of the platform. Of course he walked right through my outstretched leg, which only added to my panic. As Trevor trussed Saul's feet with towels and straps, my mind raced. What could I do?

Trevor pulled Saul to his feet and gave him an encouraging slap on the back. Saul shuffled through the gate to the edge of the launch pad.

In desperation, I flew after him and flung my arms around his waist from behind. If he was going to do this, then we'd do it together. Whatever might happen, at least I'd be right there with him.

When Saul's toes were over the edge of the platform, Trevor eased the bungee cord over the edge so that it hung in a giant loop. Holding onto Saul in back, I felt an infinitesimal tug.

Trevor began the countdown, the remaining three Brits joining in. Saul sucked in his breath and expelled it in a loud *whoof.* He spread-eagled his arms, and I tightened my grip around his waist, firmly clasping my wrist with my other hand. I buried my face in the nape of his neck as he leaned forward. Did he sense my presence at all?

When the countdown reached zero, Saul let himself fall off the platform. The wind whooshed by all around us while we plummeted. Time slowed down to a crawl. I tensed myself for the recoil.

From watching the others, I had thought we'd free-fall the entire length of the bungee cord, then be jerked up in reverse. I was surprised to feel our rapid descent slow down noticeably as we approached the end of our rope, so to speak. What appeared to observers on the platform as an abrupt recoil felt like a gentle reversal of direction to Saul and me.

He flailed his arms and legs wide, shouting in jubilation. I was jubilant that the cord hadn't broken.

Saul didn't realize that his mid-air thrashing arced us off center and toward the canyon wall. Still enjoying the rush, his wild movements increased our lateral momentum. With each swing, we came closer to the rock face. The coating of green moss that had appeared so spongy from the gondola didn't look lush from where I now hung. It probably wouldn't provide any cushioning if we smashed into the wall.

We made another round trip down and up again, Saul still flailing in wild abandon, swinging us ever closer to the canyon side. I looked up at the platform to see Trevor cupping his hands on either side of his mouth, shouting at Saul.

"Hold still! Hold still!"

But his voice was lost in the whooshing air and Saul's exultant yells. Down in the boat, the crew craned their necks, watching, waiting.

Between the rushing air and the roaring waterfall, there was no way Saul could have heard Trevor's shout. I barely heard it myself. Yet for some reason he ceased his wild movements as if just now seeing the reality of the oncoming wall. I don't know if something alerted him to the danger or if it was just lucky timing, but I didn't care as long as we stopped swinging. He tried to cross his arms over his chest but couldn't to hold them there. He let go and they hung over his head like a rag doll.

We kept cycling up and down, the lateral movement lessening each time, though we continued to arc close enough to the canyon wall to touch it. I prayed Saul's instincts wouldn't tell him to use his arm to push us away. The resulting momentum would only bring us nearer on the return swing. Thank God he remembered that, and the only arm that pushed us away from the wall was mine.

As soon as they could reach his hands, the boat crew grabbed him and pulled us down. Ian eased him down on the floor of the boat while the other crewman removed his gear. Saul just sat there, chest heaving. The rush was wearing off and reality of what he had just done started sinking in.

As for me, I felt like sobbing with relief. Whether I had been responsible or not, Saul had eluded another potential disaster. Through the treacherous van ride, boat trip, and finally the bungee jump itself, Saul had emerged unscathed.

Maybe this was one of those miracles I'd heard so much about. I allowed myself to relax.

A little.

Chapter Twenty

All the spiritual energy I'd exerted over the past few days took its toll. I felt drained and in need of renewal. With the immediate danger to Saul over, I was okay with leaving him in New Zealand while I went home to decompress. Even spirits have to take it easy sometimes, rebuild their strength.

I also wanted to see if Micaela needed any help getting settled on Seven. I really had to thank her. Her last words to me at the Welcome Center still echoed: *Everything will turn out for the good.* After bringing Saul through the bungee experience in one piece, I was finally ready to believe her.

I headed for the place that always seemed to bring me tranquility: the Jungle. As soon as the animal spirits gathered around me, tension melted away. I hunkered down to nuzzle Midnight, inhaling the scent of his warm fur. The Jungle was a respite from all my struggles to save my husband. Here I met no opposition, no disapproval, just unconditional acceptance.

"Acceptance is all around you, Judith."

Ashraf's sudden appearances no longer caught me off guard. I'd come to expect him to home in on my thoughts, even to welcome it.

I cupped Midnight's chin, dropped a kiss on his rough nose, and got to my feet. Ash stood poker-straight, but carried a large ledger in the crook of his arm: a Nubian Statue of Liberty.

"What have you got there?"

Ash shook his head and put a finger to his lips. Apparently he didn't want to discuss it yet. He gazed at me with an expectation in his eyes that I didn't understand. I squirmed, growing uncomfortable in his presence, and not knowing why.

I tried to think of something conversational to break the awkward silence, but Ash spoke first. "I am fully aware of the circumstances of your friend Micaela's passing."

We were back to that. Ash didn't pass judgment on me, but his statement resurrected the guilt I carried over my part in Micaela's death. Despite her affirmations that it was not my fault, I couldn't dismiss the thought that my own tunnel vision that brought her to that fate. I suspected Ash meant to test me in some way, but wasn't sure of the subject.

"I feel awful about it, Ash." It was the only thing I could think of to say.

He didn't reply.

"At least there's one consolation," I babbled on. "Maybe Micaela had been able to get Saul thinking about the choices he's been making lately."

Ashraf shook his head again. "I am afraid not."

I hate when people tiptoe around what inevitably turns

out to be bad news. "Just say it, Ash. Say whatever is you came here to tell me."

The expectation in his eyes softened to something akin to pity. "Judith, Saul has passed over."

I gave a little laugh. "Where'd you get that idea? I just left Saul. He's fine. I made the bungee jump with him myself. It was touch-and-go for a few minutes, but he's perfectly fine. Foolish, maybe, but fine."

"Do not do this, Judith."

I cocked my head. "What do you mean?"

"Do not continue to believe that you can arrange a soul's earthly life to your liking. It is just as I and so many others have told you. Saul's destiny was his own to live out. You could not change it no matter how much you desired to."

"But I did change it, Ash, don't you see? You were wrong about that. You, Suse J, Justin–you all tried to talk me out of interfering, but in the end, it paid off. Saul came through that ridiculous escapade without a scratch."

Ash shifted the weighty book to his other arm and sighed. I waited for his next argument in our never-ending debate. Instead, a shroud of mist eddied beside him and a figure emerged from its depths.

"Saul!"

I flew to him and threw my arms around his neck, holding on for all I was worth. His etheric body was like a warm blanket fresh from the clothes dryer. Beams of yellow light spiked out all around him.

I pushed him away to look at his face. "Saul McBride, what are you doing up Here? What has Mary Lynn done now?"

At the mention of her name, Saul looked surprised and sheepish. He glanced at Ash for–I don't know, maybe moral support, but Ash had tactfully retreated, leaving Saul and me alone in the Jungle.

Anxious to hear the whole story, I took his hand and led him to a wrought-iron bench at the base of a knoll where the animals played and basked in the sun. We sat down and several dogs came over to plant moist greetings on our knees with their snouts. A few conciliatory pats and they bounded off to resume their play.

I held Saul's hand tight, feeling the familiar calluses and rough cuticles. "Tell me what happened, please."

"I died, Jude."

"Please, Saul, no jokes."

"Who's joking?"

"But I just left you at Skipper's Canyon Bridge. You were safe."

"You were there?"

I nodded.

A smile played at the corners of his mouth. "No wonder I got such a rush from the jump."

I smiled too. "I held on to you. Could you feel me?"

"I felt safe, I know that."

"You *were* safe, Saul. Everyone kept telling me that I couldn't do anything to protect you, but I knew I would find a way."

Saul lowered his gaze to our clasped hands. The corners of his mouth turned downward and the golden glow around him faded the slightest bit.

"Jude, honey, they were right. All of them. You couldn't protect me, nor was it your job to. Isn't the fact that I'm up Here proof enough?"

I still hadn't gotten any answers. "Why *are* you here? What happened after you got in the boat?"

"I guess you didn't stick around very long, did you?"

"I left once your jump was over. May I ask what possessed you to do this thing?"

Saul cocked an eyebrow. "Do I need to spell it out?"

He sure didn't. I knew those eight letters all too well. "Never mind. Go on."

"After the boat crew got me out of the bungee gear, we took off for the dock where our van driver–"

"Trevor."

"Right. Where Trevor had set up to meet us. Anyway, the guys got me into the boat and off we went. When Trevor said we'd have the ride of our lives, he wasn't kidding. The jump itself was a piece of cake by comparison. Did you happen to notice how narrow that river was?"

Did I. "Yes, I rode out in the boat with you to the gondola station. I remember when Trevor called it the 'ride of our lives'. He should really have called it the 'ride of our deaths.'"

"Then you got a taste of what I mean. Well, the ride after the jump was even wilder. It's the highlight of the whole Skipper's Canyon experience. Lots of hairpin turns at high speed."

"I know. I was there, Saul."

He continued as if he hadn't heard me. "Even worse, the crew provides an extra thrill by executing those turns at the last possible moment. It's enough to make you lose your lunch."

Or your life. "Why do they do something so dangerous?"

Saul shrugged. "That's why they call it 'thrill-seeking,' honey."

"As if the van ride up the mountain wasn't thrilling enough."

"You got that right. So we're flying along in the boat, skimming the surface of the water and heading straight for this wall of sheer rock rising straight up a couple of hundred feet. I'm waiting for Ian–that was the boat captain's name, Ian."

I stamped my foot. "I know, Saul. Waiting for Ian to do what?"

"Waiting for Ian to turn. The wall is coming closer and I'm waiting…but he's not turning. It's looming larger and larger until it's the only thing in the world and I hear myself yelling, 'FUCK!'"

I turned my face away from the mental image of the boat smashing into the wall at a speed of God-knows-how-fast.

I squeezed his hand. "You don't have to tell me any more. He didn't make the turn."

"Oh, he made the turn, all right. Veered the boat right at the last split second. We missed the wall by inches, but we made it. Mary Lynn saw the whole thing from the dock; she went into hysterics."

I'll bet. She feared she was about to lose her meal ticket.

I fought to keep my voice even. "If you made the turn, then what happened?"

"That's the ironic part. Ian turned around to see my reaction. Apparently he got a real kick out of scaring his passengers."

Quiet, capable-looking Ian? "I wouldn't have thought that of him."

"He probably acts ultra-professional just to throw passengers off. Anyway, he never saw the boulder in the middle of the river until the boat clipped it. It was only partially exposed and you couldn't really see it until you were right on top of it. We hit and the boat turned over. And over. And over."

"Saul..."

"The damned thing cartwheeled a couple of times before exploding. They say the fireball shot up half as high as the bungee platform. It must have been quite a spectacle."

"How can you be so blasé about this? It must have

been horrible."

"It happened too quickly for me to feel any fear. I can remember flipping over with the boat and hitting the water, like slamming into concrete. That's when I left my physical body and watched the incident from a few feet above. It was pretty surreal."

I was in shock. Not only was Saul dead from this horrific accident, but he recounted it as blithely as if he'd stubbed his toe. He took this in awfully good stride. For God's sake, didn't he see that I'd failed him?

His free hand covered our clasped ones and he looked into my eyes, searching. I'd never seen him so earnest.

"You see, Jude honey? You couldn't save me, after all. Ashraf told me you insisted on trying to prevent it, but I was destined to die on that trip." A smile played at the corners of his lips. "I could have told him how hard-headed you are, but I figured spirit guides already know these things."

His face turned somber again. "He also said you were persistently warned not to interfere. Why wouldn't you listen?"

"They just tried to scare me into believing there would be all kinds of consequences if I tried to change your karma. But how could I not interfere, Saul? Mary Lynn put your life at risk. You would never have behaved so recklessly without her influence. How could you fall for her, anyway? She was only after your money."

"I thought you liked her."

"I did, until I saw her true colors. You should have

seen what she did to Micaela in the hospital."

"Oh, come on. She was nothing short of wonderful when Micaela was in the hospital. She came with me every time I visited, stayed until all hours..."

"Of course she was wonderful in front of you. It's what she did when you weren't there."

"What could she have done?"

"She sent you to get Gerry from the residents' lounge. While you were gone, she threatened Micaela and deliberately tortured her!"

"Calm down, Judith. You tend to exaggerate when you're upset."

"Exaggerate? What would you call it when someone puts alcohol into an open wound? In my book, that's torture."

"Are you saying that Mary Lynn...? No, Jude, I don't believe it. M.L. wouldn't hurt a fly."

Utterly frustrated, I slumped back on the bench. Somehow I managed to keep my voice modulated. "I used to think so, too. Then I saw what she was really like. Mary Lynn Walker would trample her own mother if it would further her cause. She was in a mental hospital once, did you know that? No, neither of us knew because she lies to everybody."

Unsure what to make of my tirade, the furrow in Saul's brow deepened. I could see him weighing the best way to handle me in my present mood. He probably thought he was now an expert at handling women.

"Okay. Let's assume she did do these things," he said. "You should have known that there was nothing you could do from up Here to change them."

I gaped at him. "I just don't understand how you could have been so blind."

"Don't make me say it, Jude."

"All right, all right. I really don't want to hear it, anyway." I sighed deeply. "Okay, so maybe I was wrong about trying to save you from your destiny. But look on the bright side: we're together now. Wait 'til you see the house we're going to–"

"Judith, will you shut up for a second and LISTEN?"

I was shocked enough to do just that. In all our married life, Saul had never spoken to me like that.

"We can't stay together." His tone was softer now.

"What are you talking about? You're up Here now; of course we're going to be together."

Saul waggled our clasped hands and leaned in toward me. "*Listen* to me, Judith. You broke the rules, okay? Ashraf warned you not to interfere, but you insisted on doing things your way. I know you meant well, honey, but you know what they say about the road to hell being paved with good intentions..."

"Saul, *what are you saying?*"

He hesitated, but the words had to be said. "By trying to change destiny, you interfered with not only my karma, but others.'"

I looked down at our hands. "I know. I feel terrible

about Micaela. I've told her that. I've told Ash that. What more can I say?"

"It's not just Micaela. It's your own karma I'm talking about. By ignoring the warnings of more highly evolved souls, you've compromised your spiritual growth. The Spirit Council has decided that you have to move down to level Six to continue your development."

I sat stunned. "What? You can't be serious."

"I am, Jude. So are they. I may be new up Here, but even a greenhorn like me could tell they mean business. They feel that you weren't as ready to reside on level Seven as they had thought. You have some serious work to do on yourself."

"But I was trying to *help* you, not hurt you."

"I know that."

"And Micaela assured me that her death wasn't my fault."

"This isn't about Micaela or me, Jude. It's about you. You screwed up one of life's most important lessons. You need to get it right before you can move forward."

I stared at him. This couldn't be happening...

Ashraf was beside me then, his dark eyes full of deep compassion. "It is true, Judith. Do not be angry with Saul for bearing this news. The Council thought it would be easier for you to hear it from him."

I looked from Saul to Ash to Saul again, feeling betrayed by two of the souls I loved most. *No good deed goes unpunished.*

"Don't give me that this-is-going-to-hurt-you-more-than-it-hurts-me crap. What exactly did I miss, Ash? What's the big, important lesson I didn't seem to learn?"

"That loving isn't always having what you want. Sometimes it means learning how to let go. Giving someone the freedom to make his own mistakes...just as you have been allowed to make yours."

The impact of his words hit me with as much force as the canyon wall I had feared Saul and I would crash into on his bungee jump. I recognized the truth and anger started to melt away.

I had closed my ears to everyone's warnings and blinded myself by a human need I should have relinquished long ago up Here. No matter how legitimate the agenda, I couldn't change the fact that some things were simply out of my control. I realized it now, but it was too late for regrets.

Ash cupped my elbow. "It is time to go, Judith."

"Go?"

"To your new residence level."

"Already? But Saul just got here…"

"You shall see him again."

"We barely had any–"

Ash cut me off. "Saul loves you enough to let you go. Be worthy of his gift."

"Can I at least say goodbye to Micaela?"

Ash shook his head. "I am sorry."

"You mean I have to leave level Seven right this minute?"

"The Council would like you relocated as soon as possible."

They couldn't get rid of me fast enough. "What am I, a leper?"

"Please, my dear. The longer we delay, the more difficult your transition will be."

Images of a previous life flickered in my head...an Amish woman shunned by her community for having relations with an Englishman. The pain of her rejection felt as vivid now as it must have been then.

"I should explain to everyone," I protested.

"They will know where you are, Judith, and why. Your friends and loved ones will come down to see you."

"But I can't go up to see them." I don't know why I bothered to voice the question. I knew what he would say. Still, I needed to hear it from his lips, to make sure that there were no loopholes I might have overlooked. Spiritual demotion wouldn't be so bad if I could come up to Seven any time I wanted. It would be almost as though I had never left.

Ash's reply was ironclad. "That is correct, Judith. You may not go up to see them."

His affirmation hit me like a tenth-round kayo, knocking the breath out of me. The chilling thought struck me that I'd end up alone and lonely on Six. Oh sure, at first everyone might come down to see me on a regular basis, but that would peter out. They would have their own lives on Seven to keep them busy. Out of sight, out of mind, you know.

As for my husband, the idea of Saul living so close yet so far from me up Here was not a very heavenly prospect. I felt like a prison inmate who could only see her spouse on conjugal visits.

The analogy was closer to the truth than I realized. I was being punished for my behavior...banished, as it were. And I had only myself to blame. How many lifetimes it had taken me to understand that it was not my place to be the world's office manager? No wonder I had so many incarnations. And that stubborn streak of mine had endured them all.

That same stubbornness continued to argue that I couldn't have been so wrong to try protecting those I love. Even now, part of me wanted to shield Saul from avoidable mistakes he might make up Here, to give him the benefit of my experience. Was that such a crime?

I guess it was.

Ash escorted me to level Six, handling the transportation himself. He said it would be swifter if he teleported us, but my guess is that he didn't trust me to get us there. He probably thought I would botch the trip on purpose, just to buy myself more time.

"You may open your eyes now, Judith," he said.

I cracked open one eye.

"Ah, come now. You are not banished to the depths of hell. You are only level below your former home."

He had a point. How bad could it be?

I opened both eyes. Six didn't look so bad, kind of a poor man's Seven. The landscape of trees and flowers lacked the intense, vivid colors of my former home, but at least they were signs of life. I thought of level Four where plants were scraggly and dried out. This was a sight better than that, even if drab monotony overlaid everything: New Mexico in winter versus Washington, DC in the fullness of spring. No disrespect to New Mexico, but it falls a little short of paradise. I prefer snapdragons instead of sagebrush. Majestic magnolia to spindly yucca. Crystal streams in place of silt-brown rivers.

Then I caught myself splitting hairs and slapped myself on the wrist. What did I have to complain about? I should be grateful I wasn't on Four, or lower. I had to stop wishing for what I'd lost, and start appreciating the Joy of Six.

But the bottom line was there was no joy to be had here. My punishment was not to reside someplace unpleasant.

It was to reside somewhere without Saul.

Chapter Twenty-One

Resigned to take my medicine like a good girl, I tried to think positively. Everything happens for a reason, even if the reason isn't clear. Someday I would understand why good intentions weren't enough to reap their own rewards.

I picked out a humble bungalow to live in and tried to brighten up the dreary interior with a few cheery decorations I asked Ashraf to bring down to me: a couple of pretty porcelain bowls, a sunny travel poster, a tabletop fountain. They helped some, but didn't quite dispel the depressing sight of the dwellings faded, peeling wallpaper, and worn-out furniture. Nothing like my aerie on high, but that was a thing of the past. It didn't matter much, anyway. I could be living in a palace and still find it lacking without Saul to share it with.

Right away, I noticed some curious distinctions between Six and Seven, such as the eerie hum coming from the woods beyond my postage-stamp yard. I'd never heard such a sound before. I mustered the nerve to venture into the woods and find the source. *Lions and tigers and bears, oh my.* The closer I got, the louder the noise became. I wouldn't have been surprised to see a Martian spaceship straight out of a fifties' sci-fi flick landing in the vacant lot nearby.

Plunk! Something fell on my head. I shrieked and brushed it off so vigorously my hair stuck out with static electricity. I bent down to examine the little green alien that had landed right on top of me, and laughed. It wasn't a Martian, only a cicada, the locust-like critter that appears once every seventeen years. I remembered them well from life on earth: the discarded wings tracked inside on the bottom of your shoes, trying to keep Max and Ginger from eating the dead ones, the endless drone of their singing always in the background.

It didn't take me long to find out that cicadas up Here don't make that only-once-in-seventeen-years appearance. Oh, no. On level Six, they're a permanent fixture. Their constant drone is just that: constant. I got used to it, though, as I imagine every other Sixer had before me. After a few days, the monotonous buzz went as unnoticed as the never-ending caws of swooping crows. The lonely sound perfectly complemented my frame of mind.

I knew I should start looking for work, but then, why hurry? I couldn't seem to muster any enthusiasm for the kind of work available on Six. Funny, neither did I have that burning desire to explore this new place like I did when I arrived on Seven, or even when Justin showed me level One. Most of the time I just stayed close to home. I developed a nodding acquaintance with my immediate neighbors, but that's where it ended.

On one side lived a seventyish woman with white hair

and the smoothest complexion I'd ever seen. Her mouth always stayed in a straight line, making her look perpetually angry. It wasn't hard to detect a lot of bitterness in her life, something I didn't need rubbing off on me.

My neighbor on the other side was a man with one of those short, military haircuts. 'High and tight,' I think it's called. He never smiled either, but always waved at me before disappearing into his house. That is, I think he waved. It looked more like a crossing guard holding up his hand as a stop sign.

Neither of them ever spoke to each other or to me. I didn't know their names and I didn't bother to find out. Something about these people said 'don't bother me.' Since they didn't exactly inspire camaraderie, I had no trouble obliging.

Loneliness began to creep over me like an invasive weed, and I missed my life on Seven all the more. Even worse, my biggest fear about visits from friends on high had come true. Out of all of them, only Ashraf had come down to see me. Not a word came from Suse J or Siobhan. Had they been instructed to avoid me for a while? Was that part of my chastisement? I was dying to ask Ashraf, but was afraid of the answer. Well, if semi-solitary confinement was a deliberate part of my sentence, it was certainly effective.

By this time, I was so hungry for a familiar face that I decided to pay a visit to Justin. I know I had promised myself to stay away from him, but times were tough. 'Beggars can't be choosers' and all that. Even Justin's perverse form of companionship seemed better than nothing. I told myself that our last disastrous encounter had been a fluke. He wouldn't dare try it again. Would he?

All right, then. If I needed to regain the ground I had lost in my spiritual evolution, I might as well begin by forgiving Justin's transgression and giving our friendship another chance. There is good in souls of all levels and maybe with patience I could bring his to the surface.

Just to be on the safe side, though, I asked Ash if I could have Melly accompany me. He brought the dog to me, saying he would pick her up later. I felt much better about being around Justin with Melly by my side. He wouldn't pull anything on me while she was around, not after the way she reacted to him last time. I put on her collar and leash and off we went.

I landed us right in Justin's front yard, relieved to see my teleportation skills hadn't gotten rusty. He loitered in his usual spot against the doorframe of his house. From the cocksure smirk on his face I could tell that he'd already learned of my recent change of venue. Word sure travels fast in the afterlife. How had he found out?

His greeting wasn't exactly warm and fuzzy.

"You just wouldn't listen, would you? I tolja you weren't cut out to be way up There." He used his own body weight to push himself away from the door and swaggered toward me. "I knew you'd be back."

He didn't show any fear of Melly. He didn't seem to notice her, even when her fur bristled and she growled. I took an involuntary step backwards.

Justin halted mid-stride. "Hey, Ms. J, you ain't afraid of me, are you?"

Hell, yes. "Of course not."

The familiar lazy smile returned and he came closer. "Good. 'Cuz I figure we'll be spending lots more time together now."

He was taking a lot for granted, which nettled me even more than the implication of his words.

"Oh, you did, huh? Listen, Justin, just because I've made some mistakes doesn't mean you and I are the same. In case you've forgotten, I'm still farther along than you in soul progression."

Mere bravado on my part, as I knew all too well that I was now one level closer to Justin's. My position in the afterlife wasn't so lofty that I couldn't fall still lower.

"Aw, Ms. J, where's the love? This is your old buddy Justin here. You don't gotta put on airs with me. I don't care if you fucked up. Let's just…enjoy each other."

He didn't touch me; he didn't have to. The tone of his voice said it all. This scenario had all the earmarks of a repeat performance of our last encounter. The urge to bolt was strong, but I pushed it away. This might be something else that happened for a reason. Even someone like Justin Caso might have something to teach me. If I turned tail and ran whenever things got a little out of hand, how would I learn from the situation?

He appeared disappointed that he had failed to

intimidate me. What he hadn't banked on was that I knew him better than he thought I did. He didn't really want me; only my fear excited him. If I stayed cool to his game, the thrill dissipated.

He lit up a smoke. This must have been Justin's concept of heaven: an endless supply of unfiltered Marlboros.

"So whadja come down Here for?"

"A friendly face. Some companionship."

Smoke sputtered out of Justin's mouth and he looked me up and down with contempt. "You little hypocrite. 'A friendly face'. You wouldn't set foot down Here if it weren't for the fact that you can't go see your goody-goody friends on Seven."

"Come on, Justin, you know that's not true. I came down to visit you lots of times when I still lived on Seven."

"Yeah? And how many times since the last visit?"

"Can you blame me, after the way you behaved?"

Justin snorted. "At least I was out there. I was honest. I dint prance around like I'd achieved fuckin' Nirvana already."

Great. Either I was almost getting raped or being read the riot act. Some choice. This was not what I came down here for.

Justin did an about-face. "Go home, Ms. J," he called over his shoulder. "Come back when you figure it out."

His front door slammed and I was alone among the brittle shrubs, more depressed than I'd been in several lifetimes. "Come on, Melly, we might as well go."

The dog's head lowered to a predatory stance and she stared up at me with teeth bared. Her low growl sounded as ominous as before...except now she directed it at me.

"Melly! What's the matter with you?"

I reached down to pet her and she snapped at my hand. The fur on her back rose higher than ever and she held her tail straight out. Her eyes never left my face.

I couldn't figure out why she acted so hostile to me. I kept a firm grip on her leash and spoke softly to her.

"Come on, girl, it's me: Judith. I'm no one to be afraid of." I pulled on the leash with the slightest pressure.

Emitting a sharp bark, Melly feinted and I dropped the leash. She positioned herself to lunge again; her growl became a sinister crooning. My only thought was to get away from her.

I backed up slowly, then turned and ran, not stopping until the reassuring hot breezes of level Six hit me. I leaned against a tree to catch my breath. Even my own dog had turned against me. Lately everything I touched turned to shit.

For some reason I didn't understand, Justin's tirade left me feeling ashamed and fragile. What did I care if he was disappointed in me? Someone who pissed on toothbrushes was in no position to pass judgment on me. Still, I could no longer deny that my self-confidence was zilch.

The only happy footnote to this whole encounter is that

Saul came down to see me soon after. His visit was a breath of fresh air. We took a long walk, then sat over coffee in the kitchen while he brought me up to date on level Seven. The afterlife agreed with him. He was lively and chatty, and the warm glow around him had grown brighter. I didn't want to spoil things by asking why he hadn't come to see me before this.

The few hours we spent together were the happiest I'd had in a long time. I dreaded the moment he would say it was time to go. So did he, and delayed it as long as possible, but of course the time came. I looked down at the dregs of coffee in my cup and fought back tears.

Saul got up and came to put his arms around me. I stood up so fast I sent my chair toppling over. I pressed close to him, and a sob escaped.

He felt the wetness on his shoulder. "Don't cry, honey. I'll be back."

I pulled back to look at him. "Will you?"

"Of course I will."

I couldn't stand it anymore... "But you waited so long to come down in the first place. Why?"

He puffed out his cheeks as though he didn't want to tell me. "Ashraf asked me to wait a while, to give you a chance to get settled first."

So I was right. I was being punished. "And now?"

"Now I can come see you whenever I want, Micaela too. Same for your friends Siobhan and–who is the other one? The tall girl whose aura is always so bright?"

Suse J had a bright aura? "Suse J."

"Right. You'll have plenty of company from now on."

I had been released from Solitary. At least now I had something to look forward to.

"Promise you'll be back soon?"

"I promise," he said. "No more long goodbyes."

Saul was as good as his word. He came down about twice a week, which more than banished my feelings of isolation on joyless level Six. Sometimes Suse J came with him; other times she came with Siobhan or by herself. I never did see her aura.

I started networking for a job. If I was going to build any kind of life here, I'd better get going. Level Six didn't have an animal compound–animal souls only reside on Seven–but there had to be something useful I could do. I just had to keep looking.

There was a small meadow full of wildflowers not far from my house, the only flowers I'd seen so far. I liked to pick bouquets, even though the blooms never lasted very long. One day, as I brought in a bunch of bachelor's buttons and asters, the white-haired woman next door hailed me.

"I see you like flowers."

I looked around to see whom she could be talking to.

"Yes, you. You like flowers?"

"Flowers?" I stuttered. "Well, yeah…I like them."

"I thought so. You're always bringing them home. Don't you know they'll be dead in a day or two?"

Her attitude turned my voice prickly. "So what? I can

always get more."

"I don't know why you bother."

Jesus, this woman was a piece of work. "They brighten up the house."

She shrugged. "If you say so. Listen, there's an opening for a flower tender in the level Six Common gardens."

Gardens on level Six? News to me. "Flower tender? You mean florist?"

"Whatever. They need someone to make sure there's enough cut blossoms ready at all times so anyone can pick up a bouquet whenever they like. Are you interested?"

Well, I'll be damned. "Am I! I'll go over right away. Thanks, er...?"

"Gert. Don't mention it. I see you with those flowers all the time and figured you might want the job."

"What about the person who's doing it now?"

"I just thought you might like to have it."

"Is it...it's your job?" Gert didn't seem the type to be interested in flowers. She acted so severe.

She nodded.

"Where are you going?"

"Nowhere. I just thought you might like to have it."

"But if you're not leaving or anything, I wouldn't want to take the job away from you," I protested.

"Do you want it or not?"

"Yes, I want it. But–

"When can you start?"

I tried to make her smile. "Is tomorrow too early?"

She didn't. "Make it the first of next week." She extended her hand as though concluding some sort of important business transaction, and we shook on it.

I took a bachelor's button from the bunch I clutched in my hand and presented it to her. She looked at me as though I was some kind of a nut and twirled it between her finger and thumb. "What am I supposed to do with this?"

Do you really want to know, Little Mary Sunshine? "Whatever you like," I said politely.

"Well, good luck to you," she said.

"Thanks."

Help certainly can spring from the most unexpected sources.

'Flower tender' turned out to be nothing more than a glorified gardener, but I didn't care; I was glad to have something to do. Plus, I had first crack at the choice flowers. Things had definitely started to look up.

Saul and I had some long-overdue talks about Mary Lynn. She had gotten over the emotional trauma of his death in record time and was in fact living with Trevor in New Zealand. Seems she had ambitions of mentoring Trevor's professional future and ultimately buying the Queenstown Tours Company.

I wasn't the least bit surprised at this, but Saul had taken her defection rather hard. Sadly, he told me about her rapid 'recovery' from grief, and I tried not to make him feel worse by rubbing it in.

"I know now that she never really cared about me," he confessed. "I was foolish enough to think my money wasn't the main attraction."

"Don't blame yourself, sweetie. She took us all in." I told him about Siobhan's previous-life connection with Mary Lynn, and what she had done. He shuddered to think that he had considered marrying the woman.

"Maybe it was a blessing that I had that boat accident," he said. "Life with someone like her would have been hell on earth."

Poor Saul. He had been only human, after all. Mary Lynn was a talented manipulator, and Saul's lack of resistance and foresight was no less than any man's might have been under the same circumstances. He was still the kind, good-hearted soul who loved me as always. Knowing that he finally saw Mary Lynn for what she was made it easier for me to accept the consequences of my own actions. Closure, if you will. Now I just wanted to let go of the whole mess.

Life on Six took on a more comfortable rhythm. My job kept me busy, if not fulfilled, and I had regular visits now from the kindred spirits who warmed my soul. But something was still missing, an emptiness I couldn't name.

Saul hit on it one day as we sat talking in the Common. Daisy petals were scattered over my lap. *He loves me, he loves me not...*

"This visiting stuff, Jude: it isn't exactly the life of eternal togetherness I once pictured for us."

"You can say that again."

"So what are you going to do about it?"

"What can I do? I know I've made some bad mistakes, but I'm trying to correct them. It just takes time."

"Are you really doing all you can, Judith?"

I peered sideways at him. He only called me Judith when annoyed with me about something.

"There's obviously something on your mind, Saul. Suppose you tell me what it is."

He searched my face. "No. That won't work."

"We have little enough time together as it is, honey. Don't waste it playing games."

"It's no game, I assure you, but I can't tell you what I have in mind. If I do, it won't do either of us a bit of good. You have to come to this knowledge yourself. True soul growth can't evolve from anywhere but within you."

"You only just arrived up Here. How is it you possess the wisdom of the ages?" I asked.

He took my hand and turned it palm up in his. In a very un-Saul-like gesture, he placed my palm against his cheek for a moment, then touched his lips to it. "No more cheating, honey. Time to play it fair and square."

He got up and walked away. Just like that. He hadn't left with his usual 'see you in a couple of days.' He hadn't said goodbye at all. I stared after him, too taken aback to move, watching him get smaller and smaller until I couldn't see him at all.

Why did everyone in my life seem to be talking in riddles? I tried to figure out what he had meant by that last remark–as if his uncharacteristic display of tenderness hadn't been enough to throw me completely off guard. I finally asked Ash for his opinion.

"What do you think he meant by 'no more cheating'?"

"What do you think he meant?" Ash countered.

"Ash, please, this isn't cognitive therapy," I wailed. "I'm asking for a little help here."

"Ah, progress already."

Chapter Twenty-Two

Progress.

Until Ashraf mentioned it, I don't think I appreciated the true meaning of the word. I knew he expected me to develop into a more mature soul, but until now I had thought it was something that happened without much effort, like an earthly body growing taller. But spiritual growth isn't passive; it's an action one takes with deliberation.

How lucky I was to have lost only one rung on the ladder. I could have ended up as a permanent neighbor of Justin's. I had a new appreciation for the earthly paths that had led me to level Seven. Before I bungled things royally, that is.

So here I sat, among bunches of wildflowers on level Six, thinking that nothing worthwhile will ever happen to me again. A puff of arid wind ruffled my hair, and then I felt it. A warm influx that started at my toes and traveled rapidly up my body to fill my head. Energy burst inside me and spread to every extremity. Colors became brighter, smells got sweeter.

The prayer surge.

It had been so long since I first experienced that

overwhelming onrush of love, I had forgotten how powerful it could be. I was glad someone down there still prayed for me. I needed all the help I could get.

Ashraf's voice resonated inside my head as if he stood right next to me. *Remember what day this is, Judith.*

What was so special about this day? Today had been the first time since my arrival up Here that I felt the prayer surge, but that hardly deemed it a national holiday.

One earthly year ago today you ceased to live in your physical body.

It was my *yarzheit* and they were saying *Kaddish* for me on earth. Had a whole year elapsed since my death? It seemed like yesterday; it seemed like forever ago.

Except this time Saul wasn't one of the mourners; he was being mourned. So was Micaela. Two lives that might not have ended so abruptly if it hadn't been for me. If I hadn't taken destiny into my own hands, Saul and Micaela would have played out their own lives, lives they had charted themselves, whether a millennia ago or last week. I'd damaged my own spiritual growth, and theirs.

Now I needed to make it right. It was too late to change fate for Saul and Micaela, but not for somebody else who doesn't stop to look before she leaps. There were probably many souls like me down on earth, people who could learn from my mistake. I wouldn't interfere in their lives–I wasn't about to make that mistake again–but if I could somehow pass on what else I've learned…

I outlined my idea to Ashraf that afternoon. He listened without comment until I finished. "It would be a *mitzvah*, Ash. I'd be working on my own spiritual growth while helping someone on earth learn from my mistakes." Some of my early enthusiasm faltered and I got the feeling I hadn't done a good job of convincing him.

Ash gestured with his palms to calm down. I realized I'd been dangerously close to overselling.

"What you are proposing is unconventional, Judith. You have already lived forty-nine incarnations. You do not have to do this again."

"I know. I want to."

"You do not understand, I am afraid. You are not entitled to another earthly life."

"What, is there a maximum, like with grocery coupons? Limit forty-nine to a customer?"

He didn't even smile. "No, there is no generically predetermined limit. You and your Spirit Council decided the limit long ago."

Again with the Spirit Council.

"Couldn't you ask them to make an exception, just this once? I *know* it will work. This is the best idea I've had since watching over Saul."

Ash opened his mouth to speak, then closed it again.

"Okay, so that idea didn't work out so well," I admitted.

I had walked right into that one, but Ash didn't take advantage, bless him.

"It is not my exception to make," he said. "You must

seek the approval of the Spirit Council on this."

"Why do they have the final say?"

Ash shook his head ruefully. "Judith, Judith. Do you not remember my teachings from orientation? Each soul has many spirit guides, some of whom comprise a panel to oversee the soul's journey through its various lives."

I had a faint recollection of Ash telling me something about spirit guides. Saul had mentioned the Spirit Council when he met me up Here. Ash was right, I hadn't paid attention, but I had heard about it somewhere else, too...

"If you feel strongly that this is the path you must travel, I will arrange a meeting for you with them," he offered.

"I'd love it if you would. I really want to do this."

"Very well. I will see to the arrangements. Await me tomorrow afternoon in front of the Hall of Reflection."

"Now, wait a minute. The Hall of Reflection is on level Eight. How can I–"

"I will secure special permission for you to travel there for this conference," he broke in. For the first time I could remember, he had interrupted me.

"How will I know which building it is?"

"You will know."

What will the Spirit Council think of me, I wondered. Would they be angry? No, such highly evolved souls would have the ready gift of forgiveness. Besides, I was coming to them with a plan to correct my recent, er...transgressions. That ought to count for something. I had to make them see the plan's potential.

So why did I feel like an alcoholic applying for a job in a liquor store?

By the next afternoon, I was a nervous wreck. I tried to lose myself in a book, but I couldn't sit still. I went outside for some air, for once grateful for the relative solitude here on Six. It saved me from having to explain to anyone where I was going and why. On Seven it would have been impossible for me to make a trip like this in secret. I wouldn't have been outside my front door for more than two minutes before someone would pass by, chatting me up and inevitably asking where I was going. *Funny you should ask...*

Things were different in the ghost town that made up level Six. Life stayed quiet and still, but people watched, always watched. I figured that out when Gert offered me the flower-tender job. I had an inkling that if my fellow Sixers found out about my level Eight dispensation, it would stir up resentment. I couldn't afford to piss off anybody else. I was lonely enough.

When the time came to meet Ash, I closed my eyes and concentrated every ounce of energy on level Eight. Under normal circumstances, if I tried to transport myself to an unauthorized upper level, I'd be going nowhere fast. Because Ashraf had obtained an exemption, all systems were go.

Even before I opened my eyes, I knew I was there. I

could smell it. I could feel it. Wisteria and warm light, familiar in some intangible way, and brand new at the same time.

My first reactions to level Seven had been much the same. I thought then that life after death couldn't get much better. Ah, but that was before I knew what existed on Eight! This was unsolicited bliss, a spiritual orgasm. I was that much closer to God.

"What do you think?"

"Oh, Ash," my voice cracked. "If level Eight is like this, how much better can Nine be?"

"That must wait for another time. Right now we have an appointment to keep."

Ash was right when he said I would know the Hall of Reflection as soon as I saw it. The stately building of Jerusalem stone commanded respect. The long flight of marble steps leading up to the dim interior reminded me of the Lincoln Memorial, though the hushed, almost reverent mood inside was more like the New York Public Library. Floor-to-ceiling bookshelves lined the walls, filled to capacity with volumes identical in size and shape. Spirits sat at round tables, reading from these books or holding whispered conversations. I had no doubt this was an environment of great learning.

Ash understood. "The Hall of Reflection has this same effect on all spirits, whether newly arrived up Here or of longer sojourn. After all, this is the place where souls develop and expand their mental capabilities."

"Really?" I only half-listened, gawking like a first-timer to the Sistine Chapel.

"It is also where spirit guides receive instruction from their master guides and teachers. I have spent many eons here, even while I have been your spirit guide, learning and growing so that I may continue to help you help yourself."

Ashraf's formal way of speaking often sounded trite, and this time was no exception, but the words made sense. The soul never stops learning, no matter how highly evolved.

He led me to the center of the hall. "Your Spirit Council has been following your journey with great love and interest, Judith. They are looking forward to this meeting."

"*My* Spirit Council, Ash? You sound like you're running for election." He started to reply, but I put up my hand. "I know, I know. They're here to help me. I get it, I promise. I was just trying to lighten things up a little."

"Spiritual nourishment is not to be taken lightly. The Council does not regard it so. Indeed, they are *your* Spirit Council. Every soul has his or her own."

Ashraf's infinite patience and tranquility put me in my place more than any spoken reprimand could.

We approached a large Lucite table. *This* is where I'm meeting the Spirit Council? The Hall of Reflection was magnificent, sure, but no more intimidating than your average high-rise office. I'd expected some elaborate Oz-like theater, not the 3M Corporation.

Two women and a man sat around the table at precisely spaced intervals; a thick ledger with a worn leather cover lay in the middle. Ashraf put his palms together and made a shallow bow before the trio, his demeanor even more formal than usual. I thought they must be deserving of great respect. Happy to oblige, but I wasn't sure what was politically correct. Bowing didn't come naturally to me. At a loss, I stuck to a simple nod. They nodded and smiled back.

I hadn't alienated anyone yet. So far, so good.

My eyes went to the large book on the table. It had a long column of names I didn't recognize etched deep into the dimpled cover. The list ended with *Judith McBride*.

Ashraf pulled out a chair for me. "Please sit."

I slid into the seat, never taking my eyes off the Spirit Council, who looked at me with equal curiosity. Nobody spoke. It felt more like a Sixties' encounter group than an important meeting to decide my immediate future. Ash didn't make any introductions, and they didn't introduce themselves. Instinct told me this wasn't rudeness; names were probably not considered essential up Here. So I privately assigned them names, mostly to distract myself from the awkward silence.

The woman who sat immediately to my left had a bookish face with clouds of fluffy, nut-brown hair and thick horn-rimmed glasses. She reminded me of Zelda, the plain Jane in *The Many Loves of Dobie Gillis*.

To her left sat the only man, a balding dude with cheeks

as round as a baby's and a vapid smile. Something about him said he wasn't all there. How could that be? Up Here no one had to live with defects of any kind.

Behind me, Ash said low, "He may appear mentally challenged to you, but be assured he is a highly evolved soul. Perhaps it is merely the way you perceive him."

I should have known that up Here what you see is not necessarily what you get. Wasn't Justin a textbook example?

The right name for this man suddenly came to me: Gordon. A dignified name to compensate for his childlike appearance.

The third Council member looked like she'd been plucked right out of the Suffragette movement and wasn't about to take crap from anyone. Her steel-grey hair was pulled back in a tight bun from a stern face. A few defiant strands flailed around her temples. She would have looked intimidating, except for the palpable love emanating from her. I could give her no other name but Grace.

She spoke first.

"We would like you to know, Judith, how proud we are of you. Your soul development has come a long way, despite this most recent lapse. That you requested this meeting reinforces our faith in your overall judgment."

Gordon spoke up with no hint of impairment, mental or otherwise. "You've often been a challenge to us by continually resisting our offers of guidance." The others chuckled in agreement.

It didn't add up. I didn't remember receiving any offers of guidance from the Spirit Council, much less rejecting them. I looked to Ashraf.

"What they say is true, Judith." He reached across the table for the ledger and held it up. "This book contains your Akashic Records, a detailed archive of all the karmic debts and lessons you have sought to fulfill throughout your many lifetimes. Though you may not remember, you have met with your Spirit Council many times before. All your past lives, including this most recent one, have been discussed and agreed upon by you and the Council."

I looked at the unfamiliar names listed above mine on the book's cover: Chin Lee, Sister Faustina, Ciara Donlon, Rachel Lapp, Leilani, David Lorenz...

"Who are all these people?"

"They are all different interpretations of Judith McBride," Ash replied. "They are the names by which you were known during your previous incarnations."

So these people weren't strangers at all. They were pieces of me.

"Over the past several lifetimes, I have sent you many messages of guidance," Ash said. "But you didn't heed them. You were not of an open mind to hear me. I often had to shout to be heard."

"I don't remember any messages," I frowned.

"You did not pay attention. I had hoped to reach you through one of your dogs, but–"

"Wait... is that how Melly ended up on level Four the

last time I was with Justin?"

"Yes, I sent her to you. I know your regard for animals, and I thought you might listen to her if you would not listen to me. Animals communicate so much better than humans. I had hoped her visceral reaction to the negative karma surrounding you would make you stop and think about what you were doing."

"I understand why she reacted to Justin the way she did, but why did she growl at me?"

"So much of your time lately has been invested in negative pursuits, you absorbed some of that negative energy. She merely reacted to it, as animals do. That is of no consequence now. What is important is that you have learned what you were destined to learn during those incarnations. You fulfilled the karmic debts you owed in those lifetimes, just as you must do so now."

The last words held an ominous note. "Okay, I danced, so now I have to pay the piper. I know I have a lot to make up for," I admitted. "That's what I came here today to discuss."

A smattering of applause went around the table at my breakthrough disclosure. This was becoming more like an Alcoholics Anonymous meeting every second. *Denial…it ain't just a river in Egypt.*

"Tell us what you've learned, Judith," Grace urged. "And what you need to learn still."

Now I felt like the beauty pageant contestant who must spontaneously answer a profound question. *Who has been the most important influence in your life, Miss Alabama? What would you like to say to the leaders of the world, Miss New York? What have you learned about karmic debt, Miss Afterlife?*

"That destiny cannot be rushed, any more than it can be changed. The blueprints of our earthly lifetimes are drawn up the way they are for a good reason."

"And what is that reason?" Zelda asked in a mousy voice, the last thing I expected out of her.

"To allow the soul to follow its own path to destiny," I said without hesitation.

Saul's words echoed in my head. *No more cheating, honey.*

"Not only is it wrong to try to cheat a soul out of fulfilling its own karma, it can be downright damaging to others."

Zelda nodded approval. "Go on."

Words tumbled over one another as I told them my idea to reincarnate. "This could save others from learning the hard way, as I had to. I want other souls to benefit from my mistakes."

Gordon scratched his cheek with stubby fingers. "That would be quite an undertaking, Judith."

"I know. But it's what I want to do."

The Council members exchanged glances.

Gordon spoke for all of them." This is a highly unusual request. Level Six spirits are not entitled to another physical incarnation until significant soul growth has been achieved here in the celestial dimension."

A jumble of emotionally-charged defenses bubbled up. I swallowed them and counted to five. "I realize that. Which is why I'm asking you to make an exception in my case. I believe I can do better work on my development in an earthly life."

"Another exception, Judith?" Zelda questioned. "We granted you one to allow you to travel here for this meeting. Now you are asking to be allowed to reincarnate. Shouldn't you learn to walk before you run?"

I had no answer to that. There wasn't much more I could say to convince them, anyway. Either they would let me or they wouldn't.

Grace came to my rescue. "You do realize, surely you must realize, that if your request is granted and you reincarnate, you will further delay your opportunity to reside on the same level as Saul."

I was grateful to her, not just for smoothing over an awkward moment, but for what she said about Saul. She knew how important it was for me to be with him, and she wanted to make sure this time I thought everything through before I jumped headlong into another life. It said a lot for her compassion.

"I've thought about this long and hard, believe me. I know it would be faster to stay up Here and work my way back to level Seven and Saul. But who would benefit other than me? No one. That seems rather selfish to me, and I think I've been selfish enough for a few millennia."

The Council exchanged glances again.

"Besides, I'll be with Saul eventually."

I didn't seem to be making a very good case for myself. Grace folded her hands on the table and leaned forward.

"Why is Saul more important to you than the other souls you have loved in all your lives?"

Whew, I didn't see that one coming. "I–I'm not sure how to answer that. Perhaps it's because we were together so recently. I just feel that I belong with him." I hoped that was the answer they looked for.

Grace looked down at her hands. Zelda removed her glasses and polished them on the hem of her robe. Gordon looked at me, silent.

My voice took on a pleading note. "I know in my heart that reincarnation is the right thing to do. I *need* to do this."

Mutely the Council consulted with one another. The seconds dragged by, but I was at peace now. Whatever happened now was for the best.

"Very well, Judith," Gordon said.

My face lit up and I started to come out of my chair.

Gordon held up his hand. "However, there is one thing we would like you to do first."

Right. There's always a catch. I sat back down and looked from one to the other.

"We would like you to review your past lives. After that, if you still wish to reincarnate, if you truly feel that another earthly life is the right path for you, then by all means, go."

That came as a relief. "Sure! That ought to be interesting."

Zelda stood up. "Come with us."

She led the way to a far corner of the great room with a blank space cleared on the wall, the only unoccupied space in the entire hall. In front of it sat a La-Z-Boy recliner.

"Make yourself comfortable," she invited.

Hey, this wasn't bad at all. "Got any popcorn?"

Another look passed among the three Council members. Too late I remembered what Ashraf said about not taking this lightly.

I sat down in the recliner and extended the footrest, thinking how much more natural the situation seemed for watching a Mel Brooks movie instead of Lifestyles of the Dead and Famous–or Not So Famous, as the case may be. But who knows? Maybe I had been Theda Bara, Eleanor Roosevelt...or Tokyo Rose.

The dim light inside the hall dimmed further and multi-dimensional images appeared on the blank wall. With no beam of light, no hum of video equipment, no discernible speakers or amplifier, it was impossible to tell where the holographic pictures ended and I began.

Stories began unraveling and I saw myself in many different bodies. I was a nineteenth century Chinaman with a single braid down my back and a conical straw hat, hacking away with a scythe at a crop in the fields. I was an Austrian nun in full habit complete with pinched wimple, leading a group of schoolchildren through the courtyard of an ancient abbey. A crack-head woman with long matted hair and a gaunt face, being led to jail in crude handcuffs. It seems I had gone in search of my next fix and left my infant son alone in his crib where he suffocated in his own vomit. I was a thirteen-year-old Mennonite girl coming to grips with an arranged marriage to a widower my father's age with children older than I. A lovely, sarong-clad Polynesian girl walking bravely up a mountainside amidst a throng of villagers, trying to remain composed but faltering in my step now and then. I had been found guilty of an adulterous liaison with a village elder and was about to be punished for my sin. The fact that the man had forced himself on me didn't seem to matter. The other elders had taken his word over mine and now I went to be thrown off a cliff for my crime...

The Renaissance...colonial America...World War II...the Great Depression...men...women...children. I watched myself live forty-nine lives as individual as snowflakes, some happy, some tragic, some mundane. In one life I emptied chamber pots; in another I lived as a privileged New York debutante. I was a celebrated diva at La Scala and a waitress at Howard Johnson's. I was the Seminole medicine man of a sixteenth-century village in what is now Florida, headmistress of a private girls' school in Edinburgh, a sweat-shop foreman on New York's lower east side, a vaudevillian, and a sixth-grade math teacher. Some lives were long while others were all too brief. The achievements of some brought a proud smile to my face, while the injustices of others brought tears. And in between there were just as many lives which prompted nothing more than a shrug for their obscurity.

The last images faded and the hall slowly illuminated. It was a humbling experience. I had endured so much in many of the lives that you'd think I'd never have reincarnated again, but I kept going back for more. At least no two tragic lives ever followed consecutively. A happy— or at least uneventful—life always fell in between, a rejuvenation to prepare for the next life's darker challenges. I had a happy ending: my most recent life, the one I shared with Saul.

I got up from the recliner and stretched. The Council waited for my reaction to *Past Lives: The Movie*.

"Well?" asked Grace.

"I've been through a lot." I was a *maven* at stating the obvious.

Gordon agreed. "We wanted to make sure you understand what may be in store if you take on another earthly life."

"You may find more than you bargained for," added Zelda. "Are you prepared for that?"

I saw their point. The blueprint for this next life might be harmless, but the actual path I end up taking could spell trouble. There's no way to predict free will. Could I handle being thrown off another cliff, or burned at the stake?

No more cheating, honey...

No more running away. "I'll take my chances."

"Very well, Judith. If this is your wish, then go ahead with it."

"And take our love with you," added Grace.

Impulsively, I hugged Zelda. She kept her arms glued to her sides as if afraid I would pry them apart. Some people are just not touchy-feely, even up Here. Then I hugged Gordon, who squeezed me back with the all the vigor of an eight-year-old. Finally Grace, who ceased being the stern matron and became a grandmother smelling like just-baked cookies. Hers was the best hug of all.

Over her shoulder, Ash materialized out of the shadows.

"From the expression on your face, I need not ask if your request has been granted," he smiled, happy for me.

"Ash, would you ask Saul to come down to Six say goodbye to me?"

"Of course, my dear. I shall ask Micaela, as well. And Judith...remember that I will still be with you on earth."

"We all will," Gordon added.

I couldn't forget my spirit guide who had seen me through so much. I put my arms around Ashraf. "Thank you," I whispered.

I turned to the Council. "Thanks to all of you. You don't know how much this means to me."

Zelda smiled. "I think we do."

"And Ash, I promise the next time you try to tell me something, you won't have to shout."

Everyone laughed, though I hadn't meant it to be funny.

"We shall see, Judith. We shall see," Ash replied.

I took a deep breath. It looked like I would have my Mulligan, after all. This time I was determined to get it right.

Chapter Twenty-Three

I met twice more with the Council to work out a life plan appropriate for my current spiritual status, yet with ample opportunity for further growth. I wouldn't be driving down Rodeo Drive in a Rolls, but I wouldn't be panhandling on Skid Row, either. No matter what kind of life I led, I would be reincarnating into someone who would always be on the lookout for ways to grow spiritually.

For these meetings, the Council came down to level Six. My temporary travel pass to level Eight had been a single admission, not a season ticket. I was sure this was a deliberate attempt on the Council's part to keep me grounded. Visit level Eight more than once, and I might get delusions of grandeur. I could have told them that would not happen, that I had complete control over my impulses, but they never brought it up so I didn't, either.

I tried to ignore the curious stares of the other Sixers at the library where we met. They wouldn't be able to reincarnate for a long time and I could see they wondered why I rated a new life. It wasn't going to be a cakewalk, but what worthwhile life is? I couldn't wait to get started...

I lay on the rather lumpy couch in my living room,

trying to concentrate on a book when someone knocked on the front door.

"Who is it?"

My husband's deep voice answered. "It's us."

True to his promise, Ash had told them about my plans and to see me right away.

I flung the paperback aside and flew to the door. Saul bustled in with a radiant Micaela. Her secret feelings for Saul manifested in exceptional beauty. Had loving Saul made me look so beautiful?

I touched cheeks with Micaela. "We heard about your plan," she bubbled. I couldn't get a word in edgewise as Saul hugged and kissed me. I was as flustered as the guest of honor at a surprise party.

I left them in the living room while I went to the kitchen to get some Cokes. In the few minutes I was out of sight, Saul's light mood darkened. When I came back, he squirmed on the well-worn sofa in search of a more comfortable spot. Micaela's perkiness had taken a noticeable nosedive, as well.

I knew the reason. The McBride house they both knew on earth was nothing like this place.

"I know...the springs are pretty well shot. What a difference one level makes..."

Saul and Micaela exchanged looks. *She's putting up a good front. Celestial demotion can't be as trivial as she'd like us to believe...*

"Hey, come on, don't look so downcast. I didn't ask

you here for a pity party. This reincarnation is a good thing."

"But why, Jude? Why do you want to put yourself through that?" asked Micaela.

"Hey, who's to say I won't be sitting pretty in a Beverly Hills mansion or something? I'll put myself through that any day."

"Are you sure you aren't trying to punish yourself?"

"Come on, Mic, you know me better than that."

"I know you pretty well, too," Saul put in. "You've always taken on guilt that's not yours. Now you think it's your fault that Micaela and I died when we did."

"This isn't about guilt. It's about responsibility. There's a difference, and I don't think I really understood that before."

Saul didn't look convinced. In fact, the pair of them looked downright doleful, but I refused to allow my *bon voyage* to take place under a cloud of melancholy.

I set down the tray of drinks on the coffee table and put my hands on my hips. "Now listen, you two. I've been up Here a little longer than either of you, so you're going to have to trust me on this. Reincarnation is not something I want to do, it's something I must do. For my own peace of mind."

"But it will take you that much longer to regain the spiritual ground you've lost," Micaela protested.

"I know it will. I figure I have it coming, but you'll see, the time will fly. Before you know it, we'll all be together again, and when we are, I will be a better person for having done the work, a more complete soul."

I looked from Saul to Micaela to Saul again. "Guys, don't do this, okay? I want a happy send-off."

Saul looked down at the floor. Micaela said, "If this is what you want, Jude, then you know we're behind you."

"You could have fooled me."

"We're just afraid you might be jumping too fast into reincarnation without giving yourself a chance up Here," Saul explained.

"The way you jumped off Skippers Canyon Bridge?"

Saul's eyes narrowed.

"Sorry. That was uncalled for. I know you're being serious. But I'm not jumping this time. I don't think I'll jump into anything ever again. I've done a lot of soul searching." I got a thin smile. "Seriously, I've given this a good deal of long, hard thought, and the Spirit Council wouldn't have agreed if they didn't think it was right for me."

A sudden weariness hit me. Why did I always have to defend my motives? First to the Council, now to my husband and best friend. The visit hadn't turned out the way I had anticipated. I suppose that's the way life is. It's a series of twists and turns you don't always plan for and can't possibly avoid. After all, that's how this whole thing got started.

Sighing, I took the tray of untouched glasses back to the kitchen. My own exuberance had drained away, a sure sign that Saul and Micaela's doubts had enshrouded all my positive energies. That was the last thing I needed right now.

I didn't want to part on such an ungratifying note, but the party was over. They needed to get on with their own lives up Here and not worry about me. They had their own work to do. And so did I.

So did I.

The Reincarnation Pavilion spanned the length of half a football field, a cross between an H.G. Wells time machine and a misplaced metal detector. I peeked inside the tunnel's wide entrance like an actress checking the house before she goes on stage. A bright wall of light undulated like molten gold.

Ashraf joined me there in his noiseless way. "The proverbial light at the end of the tunnel?" I asked.

He grinned broadly, teeth gleaming white against his Nubian complexion. "It is no proverb, Judith. This is for real."

"Judith?"

I turned around and there stood Saul.

"I couldn't let you go without saying goodbye."

My eyes stung. "I thought we did that yesterday."

"That wasn't my idea of goodbye. Honey, we didn't mean to upset you–"

I put my fingers over his lips. "You don't have to say another word, Saul."

"But I do. I know how much this means to you and, well...I just want you to know I believe in you."

His face blurred in my vision. He touched his finger to a teardrop running down my cheek and put it to his tongue. "Sweet."

I grabbed the front of his shirt and pulled him to me. "See you in a little while, huh?" I whispered into his ear.

"Right. A very short while. By the way, I forgot to tell you yesterday–"

"What?"

"You're not going to believe this, but my father is changing his name back to Mandelberg."

I stepped into the tunnel cautiously, half expecting lights to blink and buzzers to sound because I'd forgotten to take off my chain link belt. Nothing happened, only the wall of light at the other end undulated faster as I walked toward it. Halfway through the tunnel, I turned for one last wave. Ashraf's dazzling smile was the last thing I saw before my conscious memories were purged. The wall of light beckoned, and I quickened my step.

Epilogue

Somewhere in a quiet suburb....

The doorbell chimed. Destiny barked and scrambled joyously to the front door.

McKenna Mandel's rapid typing halted in mid-sentence. "Shit. Why is it always when I'm on a roll?" She tucked a stray wisp of blonde hair behind one ear and glanced out the window. The UPS courier stood on the front stoop with a package in his hands. "Double shit." She pushed the rolling chair back from the computer keyboard and went to open the door. "Hello, Fred."

"Hey there, Ms. M. Lookin' good this morning," he drawled, eyeing her up and down with frank appreciation.

She knew it was irrational, but interactions with Fred always left her with an uneasy feeling. More than once she'd considered complaining to UPS and insisting on a new courier, but she was reluctant to admit that his little ingratiations bothered her. She disliked feeling vulnerable even more than she disliked him.

McKenna snatched the digital receiving log from his hand. Damn him and his smarmy flirtations. Even if she wasn't happily married to Jon, did this slob—with his slick hair and grimy fingernails—think she'd find him attractive?

Even the pruny pads of his fingers, as if he'd stayed too long in the tub, repulsed her. Judging from his overall appearance, though, McKenna doubted that he saw a bathtub very often.

She scribbled her name in the rectangular window with the magnetic pen, and reached for the thick flat envelope in his hand. He tightened his grip on it, starting the mock tug-of-war he liked to play with her. His next predictable move would be to grab her hand and refuse to let go. McKenna wrested the envelope away before he had a chance, silently vowing that if he pulled this one more time, she'd get on the phone to his supervisor.

Pleased with the barely contained infuriation he had roused in her, Fred yawned out loud, not bothering to cover his mouth. He gave McKenna a knowing leer. "See ya around, Ms. M. Yeah, I'll be seein' ya."

The hell you will... "Goodbye, Fred." She shut the door and made a gagging face. The sight of his nicotine-stained teeth was not one she relished so soon after breakfast. In fact, her stomach felt downright queasy. She turned away from the door, but hesitated and dead-bolted it, just for good measure.

Shivering off the seedy aftermath of Fred, McKenna took a carving knife from the wooden sheath on the kitchen counter and sliced open the envelope. A sheaf of papers slid out and fell to the floor in disarray.

"Shit," she muttered for the third time in five minutes. She bent to gather them, her eyes drawn to the topmost page.

Virtually illegible chicken scratches had been scrawled over her carefully prepared cover letter. *Thank you for your submission... afraid it's just not right for us...certain you will have no trouble placing it elsewhere...*

Another specious rejection. She'd accumulated quite a collection of them. Just once she wished an editor would come right out and say, 'your plot line sucks' or 'your style is boring.' At least then she'd know why he didn't want the piece.

McKenna flung the pages to the floor. The story had gone out a dozen times to a dozen different literary magazines, both domestic and abroad...and nothing.

She pushed the damp bangs off her moist forehead and made her way back to the spare-bedroom-turned-home-office. Just as she sat down at the computer, her queasy stomach progressed to full-fledged nausea. She clapped a hand over her mouth and fled to the bathroom.

Although short lived, the spasm left her weak and sweaty. As she collapsed back into the desk chair, Destiny's tail thumped on the floor beside her. She reached down to pet the dog who always curled up under the desk while she worked.

The stray Labrador retriever, black as midnight, had come wandering into her yard one day last summer. He spied McKenna through the window, propped his front paws on the glass, and barked.

Unable to resist any animal, she answered his summons and went outside to investigate. Kneeling down beside him, she offered the back of her hand for the large dog to sniff. He ignored the hand and wriggled into the open space between her knee and torso, nestling his head under her neck. Used to dogs taking to her, McKenna found this one to be a little different. He acted as though she was a long lost friend. The black tail became a grey blur as it wagged furiously.

McKenna had been instantly and incurably smitten. The timing couldn't have been better; Jon had been talking for weeks about getting a dog to accompany him on his morning runs. She had no trouble convincing him to keep the Lab. She made a perfunctory attempt to learn if he already had an owner but knew that she could not give him up. When no one responded to the newspaper ads and locally posted signs, she relaxed. The dog was theirs.

Deciding fate had brought them together, she named him Destiny. His company was just what a solitary writer needed; never more so than now when McKenna was discouraged about the whole business. She'd been a successful freelancer for about five years, earning more than she had at her day job as a research analyst. Her journalistic achievements gave her the confidence to try writing fiction, but the novel she'd recently started fought her every inch of the way. It took forever to grapple every chapter from her normally fertile imagination. This morning's prolific spurt had been a rarity, which is why she especially resented Fred's interruption that only brought her more bad news.

She rolled the chair toward the desk and hit the *print*

button on the computer. The laser printer hummed and clacked as the pages she had written that morning slid into the receiving tray. Reading over her work, what she had earlier considered good now seemed amateurish and dull.

She balled up the pages and tossed them into the wastebasket, then grasped the computer keyboard and stabbed the backspace key, holding it firmly down as it gobbled up the words on the screen like a literary Pac-man. Back to the drawing board...

She turned away from the discouraging sight of the empty screen and stared out the window, her mood about as bleak as the dreary November day outside. *Maybe I'm coming down with something. I feel so drained.*

The phone jangled, startling her.

"Hello?"

"Hi, Mac."

McKenna smiled at the nickname her friend Liz had bestowed on her. She was used to the inevitable comments on her unusual name, after her mother's favorite beach in Hawaii and a nod to her Gaelophile father. Surprisingly, no one had ever called her anything but 'McKenna' until she and Liz met in college. Declaring that 'McKenna' sounded pompous, Liz dubbed her 'Mac' and the nickname stuck. Now the only ones who called her 'McKenna' were her grandmother and telemarketers.

"How's it going, Lizard?"

"Can't complain. You?"

McKenna gave a sardonic *humph*. "Fine, until I got

another rejection. Via UPS, no less. Now I can experience the agony of defeat even faster."

"I didn't think editors bothered to send rejections by UPS."

"They don't, but this one's from the U.K. so I had sent a return waybill with my UPS account number on it. It's easier than traipsing to the post office for international postage coupons, plus I can track the delivery."

Liz paused. "Uh huh. Listen, my anal friend, I have a proposition that might cheer you up. Sylvia and I are going to the Circle of Life Center tonight and want you to come with us. One of their resident psychics is going to channel the Buddha."

"Channel the Buddha?"

"I know, it sounds a little weird to me, too, but Sylvia's heard her and says it's amazing."

"You have got to be kidding me."

"Nope. The audience even gets to ask Buddha questions. Come with us. It'll be fun and get your mind off work for a few hours."

McKenna's eyes slid to the blank computer screen. What the hell. She certainly wasn't getting anything accomplished on the creative front today. "Sure, why not. Maybe Buddha can tell me if I should just give up on this book altogether."

"It's not going well?"

McKenna snorted. "That's putting it mildly. And then that UPS creep showed up to completely ruin my day."

"Again? You should really get rid of that guy, Mac."

"I am rapidly approaching that point."

"So what do you say, are you with us?"

"Count me in."

"Great. We're meeting at my house, seven o'clock."

"Okay. See you then."

McKenna dropped her car keys on the small desk by the telephone and listened for signs of life from the den. The house was quiet, a single table lamp the only illumination. Jon had already gone to bed and she knew Destiny would be sprawled out next to him, head on McKenna's pillow.

The evening at the Circle of Life Center had been interesting, but contrived. Still, it was fun having an evening out with the girls. She hadn't done that in a long time. It had been rejuvenating, but now McKenna could feel her energy ebb all at once. She poured herself a glass of water, switched off the lamp, and trudged upstairs to join Jon and Destiny.

When the doorbell rang the next morning, McKenna was still in her bathrobe, sipping a second Coke. For some reason, the coffee she guzzled every morning soured her stomach today, and she hoped the Coke syrup would soothe the queasiness.

Ever so slightly, she lifted one of the slats of the office window blinds drawn against the morning sun and peered sideways, trying to identify the early visitor. She could only see his brown-shirted back, but she'd recognize that greasy hair anywhere.

At that precise moment, Fred whipped his head around and stared fixedly at the covered office window.

McKenna dropped the slat as if it burned her fingers and jumped back. Automatically, she wrapped the neckline of her robe a little higher on her neck. She tiptoed to the window again and carefully parted the slats a tiny bit to peek out. She was sure he couldn't see her, yet he leered at the window as though he knew she watched him. He grinned and slowly ran his tongue across his upper lip.

Disgusted, McKenna dropped the slat again and took stock of her choices. She could pretend she wasn't home, but then she'd miss the delivery. What if he brought a long-awaited acceptance instead of the umpteenth rejection? On the other hand, answering the bell meant another unpleasant encounter that seemed bound to sicken her already weak stomach.

Curiosity won. Of the two evils, putting up with him for a few minutes was the lesser. She strode purposefully to the front door, anxious to get it over with.

She shielded herself as much as she could behind the door as she opened it. "Yes, Fred?"

His grin was oily. "Got a box here for you, Ms. M. Looks like it's from Amazon." He turned the cardboard package over and around in his hands, examining the shipping label.

Where the hell did he get off? The contents of her

deliveries were no business of his. Her temper flared, but with effort she kept it in check. "Uh...yes, I ordered the new Wendy Sand Eckel novel."

"Yeah? What's it called?"

As if he would know who Eckel was. "*After May*," she gritted out and tried to snatch the box out of his hands.

Quicker than she, Fred held it out of her reach. "Uh, uh, uh," he chided. "No tickee, no wash." He waggled the receiving log in front of her face, just far enough out of her reach so that she had to emerge from behind the door to sign it. "You show me your box, and I'll show you mine."

Anger exploded in her belly, crowding out the nausea. She stepped out from behind the door, uncaring that the belt holding her robe together had loosened, and looked Fred straight in the eye. His mouth had just begun to purse in a silent whistle when McKenna grabbed the package out of his hand and slammed the door shut. She smiled in triumph as Fred cried, "Hey! You dint sign for it. Hey, Ms. Mandel!"

The doorbell pealed again, but McKenna ignored it. She took the package to the kitchen, hearing Fred's insistent rapping on the office window. "Hey, Ms. Mandel! You gotta sign for it. C'mon, I'll get in trouble!"

McKenna marched to the window and yanked on the cord that raised the blinds. With a delicious sense of puissance, she gave Fred the finger and laughed as his eyes narrowed into slits. She let the blinds drop and returned to the kitchen with a little spring to her step. The day just might turn out to be okay, after all.

Eventually–much later than McKenna would have predicted–the window rapping stopped. Destiny came over and jumped three times in a circle, his way of asking to go outside in the fenced yard. She opened the back door for him and listened to the gratifying roar of the UPS truck as Fred gunned it up her steep driveway. Good.

She smiled at Destiny and closed the back door, unaware that Fred had braked his truck at the top of the hill and sat glaring down at McKenna's office window.

McKenna pulled *After May* from the box and skimmed the first chapter, tempted to sit down with it right away, but she clapped the book shut. *Business before pleasure.* She went through her email and updated some website information, a task that stretched out into an ordeal she hadn't planned for when the program crashed. A good two hours slipped by before she remembered that Destiny was still outside. He usually scratched at the back door mere minutes after she let him out, but she was glad that he was burning up some of that endless energy.

She gave up on the computer and ran upstairs to throw on some shorts and a tee shirt. At the back door she called for Destiny, but the dog didn't come running. She stepped out on the patio and called again. She scanned the expanse of yard for a glimpse of black fur, but saw only the trees and grass as usual. A cold knot took shape in the pit of her stomach, and she went to the edge of the cement walkout and looked around the corner of the house.

Destiny lay on his side, his heaving chest the only movement. McKenna flew to him and gently lifted his head. His questioning eyes looked into hers before they rolled upwards and his body relaxed.

Panic started to envelop her, but she suppressed it enough to make a fairly coherent call to the emergency vet clinic. But she knew in her heart it was already too late.

The necropsy report listed cyanide poisoning as the cause of death. Dr. Reed had gently questioned McKenna as to how the dog might have ingested the poison. She told him they kept anything toxic securely out of Destiny's reach, either in the garage or in closed cabinets. They didn't even own anything containing cyanide or its derivatives. She had no answers, until two days later when Fred rang her doorbell.

She knew her tear-splotched face and swollen eyes were bound to elicit a snide remark, but in her grief she didn't care. "What do you want, Fred?"

His voice was oddly solicitous. "Why, Ms. M, what's the matter?"

McKenna dabbed at her runny nose with a wadded tissue. "My dog, um, passed away." Just saying the words threatened her shaky composure.

"Destiny?"

McKenna nodded.

"Then I guess you won't be needing this." He held out his hand. On the open palm lay Destiny's collar and ID tags.

McKenna reflexively stepped back. "You! You did it. You killed my dog!"

Fred tipped his head back and laughed. "Me? I'm just bringing your dog's collar I found by the side of the road."

"You sonofabitch, you did it. I know you did."

Fred's face suddenly sobered. "Yeah? What else do you know? Dontcha notice anything funny? About me?"

"There's nothing funny about you, Fred. Now, since you're not in uniform, you're obviously not here on UPS business. So either tell me what you want or get out."

"So you did notice. Yeah, I'm not in my uniform. And you know why?"

McKenna blew her nose and didn't answer.

"Cuz I fucking *lost my job*, that's why. Cuzza you!"

McKenna looked up. "What the hell are you talking about? If you lost your job, I'm afraid I can't take credit for it."

"I *told* you I had to get my log signed, but no, you just took your fucking package and dint care. When I got back to the station without a delivery signature, the bastards fired my ass. Said it was the last straw."

McKenna perked up at this news. "Good! I'm glad they fired you. And now I'm going to put your sorry ass in jail!"

Fred laughed again. "Go ahead, lady, knock yourself out. Alls I did was return a dog collar to its rightful owner. You got nothing to pin on me."

Despite all the emotions vying for space in her brain,

intellect told her he was right. She had no proof he poisoned Destiny. He'd never made any threats or exhibited inappropriate behavior…to the dog, at least.

Fred watched her carefully and knew he had her. Free of the looming threat of getting fired, he didn't bother to censor himself. He cupped McKenna's cheek with a grimy hand, then patted it lightly as he turned to leave. "See ya around, Ms. M."

McKenna recoiled at his touch and retreated inside. Dry-eyed, she shut the door.

Jon was livid when McKenna told him at dinner about Fred's special delivery. "That bastard's not going to get away with this."

McKenna pushed around uneaten peas on her plate with her fork and sighed. "There's really nothing we can do. We have no evidence to back up an accusation like that. Besides, it's not exactly homicide. No one will care that he killed a dog."

Jon stared at his wife. "I can't believe I'm hearing this from you. I would think you, of all people, would be out for blood."

She started mashing the peas with her fork. "I know. I'm a little surprised myself. At first I wanted to get back at him, to hurt him as much as he hurt me. It was all I could do to keep from raking my nails as hard as I could down his smirky goddamned face. But after he left, I thought about it. Hurting him won't bring Destiny back. Revenge would just put us on the same lowlife level as he."

Jon continued to stare at her. "Okay, who are you and what have you done with my wife?"

The mashed peas before her eyes swirled into a green blur. *God, I'm so hormonal these days.* "Oh. So I decide to take the high road and you wonder where the usual, bitchy McKenna went? Is that what you think? This isn't easy for me, Jon. I thought you'd be proud of me."

"I *am* proud of you, just a tad surprised that you're taking it so calmly. You have to admit, Mac, it's not your typical reaction."

McKenna sighed again. "I know, but Fred *wants* to piss me off. Anger and retaliation are what he's after, but I'm not going to give it to him. Besides, I kind of figure that getting caught up in an endless cycle of vengeance and anger isn't very healthy."

Jon rose from his chair and came around to McKenna's. He took her face in his hands and planted a loud smack on her lips. "McKenna Mandel, you never cease to amaze me."

McKenna smiled up at him, a squished smile because his hands still held her face. "In a good way, I hope."

Jon kissed her again, tenderly this time. "In a very good way."

Every day without Destiny was difficult, but McKenna knew that with each one, the hurt lessened just a wee bit. She gathered up all Destiny's toys and equipment to donate to the animal shelter, everything but the collar Fred had taunted her with. This she kept on the windowsill above the kitchen sink where she could see it every day, a memorial to Destiny. Admittedly, it also served as a reminder that she'd beaten Fred at his own game.

Several weeks went by before UPS rang the Mandels' doorbell with a delivery. Funny, McKenna wasn't expecting anything; Jon must have ordered something online. She opened the door to the familiar brown uniform, but its wearer was as unlike Fred as anyone could be.

The tall, slender man smiled politely. "Good morning." His singsong voice pointed to a foreign ethnicity.

McKenna couldn't help but smile back. "You're new, aren't you?"

"Yes, madam. I have been on this route only a short time. The previous courier...er, left rather suddenly."

Damned right he did. "Yes, I had heard that." She extended her hand. "I'm McKenna Mandel."

He shook her hand with a single pump. "A pleasure, Madam Mandel. My name is Nabil."

"Have you been in this country long, Nabil?"

"Oh, yes. I have been around practically forever." He looked past her, through the open door into the vestibule. "Forgive me, madam, but UPS couriers receive a list of residential stops with dogs on our routes. It is just a precaution, so drivers are not taken by surprise. According to the report I received, you own a dog, a Labrador retriever, I am told. I cannot help but notice the absence of a dog here."

At the unexpected reference to Destiny, McKenna's eyes stung.

Nabil noticed her reaction immediately. "Ah, Madam Mandel, I did not mean to upset you."

McKenna waited to answer until she knew her voice wouldn't crack. "It's all right. I lost my dog not long ago, that's all."

"He ran away?" he asked in a sympathetic tone.

"No." Compelled by his kindness, she told him the truth–sort of. "He died. Someone fed him poison."

Nabil's brows furrowed. "Who would do such a terrible thing? Did you have the slime arrested, I hope?"

Tempted to spill the whole story, she resisted. "I have my suspicions who did it, but no proof. Besides, he'd love nothing better than to see how deeply he's wounded me. So I'm not going to give him the satisfaction. And in the long run, it doesn't really matter. The culprit will answer for it eventually. Of that I'm certain."

"You sound like a woman of great faith, madam."

"Without faith, what have you got?"

Nabil completed his delivery and clambered into the UPS truck parked at the top of the Mandels' driveway. He stowed the receiving log in its compartment under the dashboard, then retrieved a metal box from the floor behind the driver's seat. He unlocked it and lifted out a thick ledger with a tooled leather cover. He opened it and carefully leafed through the gilt-edged pages until he found the one he sought.

He took a pen from his shirt pocket and wrote with an elegant hand on a page toward the back of the book. When he finished, he closed the book and smoothed his hand over the cool leather. He carefully replaced it in the metal box and put it back behind the seat.

His smile, as he started the engine and shifted the truck into gear, was dazzling.

About the Author:

A writer for life, author Cynthia Polansky is a cross-genre novelist whose refusal to settle for the ordinary translates into stories that are food for thought. A professional writer/editor since 1993, she uses her distinctive writing style to satisfy the reader hungry for something different from the ubiquitous romances and mysteries. She is the award-winning author of two published novels and four nonfiction dog-breed books (under the name Cynthia P. Gallagher). She has served on the board of the Maryland Writers Association, and is a member of the Women's National Book Association and the Dog Writers Association of America. Committed to the cause of literacy and education, Cynthia enthusiastically serves as a Writing Center tutor at the United States Naval Academy. Visit her website at *www.cynthiapolansky.com*.

Book Group Discussion Questions

1. How does Judith demonstrate her controlling nature, while alive and in death?

2. What is the meaning behind Suse J's name?

3. What examples can you find of double entendre language the author used?

4. What similarities and differences are there between Judith's heaven and the afterlife as portrayed in major religions? Your own version of heaven?

5. Why is Judith so reluctant to heed the warnings of her friends and spirit guide about intervening with earthly events?

6. Why would spirit Denise choose to keep her unattractive appearance ("…bushy eyebrows, pitted skin…") on the Other Side?

7. How many afterlife-relevant puns can you find in the text?

8. When Judith appeals to a sleeping Micaela to talk Saul out of his New Zealand trip, she assures her friend that the next morning she wouldn't remember that Judith's spirit had communicated with hers as it did. So why does Micaela tell Mary Lynn on the phone that Judith had come to her in a dream?

9. What examples demonstrate that Judith's soul is not as highly evolved as she thinks?